cinnamon saviors

patient 247

CARMEN RICHTER

Trigger warning

This book deals with the following issues:

- Graphic descriptions of medical conditions (including open wounds)
- Medical trauma
- Body dysmorphia
- Fatphobia (both internalized and external)
- Secondary character's struggle with domestic violence

Also, please note that the heroine in this book is one of many victims of the misogynistic, fatphobic American healthcare system. Her pain and obvious serious medical condition are continually overlooked, ignored, and minimized, and she's also told multiple times that weight loss surgery will be a magic cure for her problems. The scenes describing this are graphic and meant to be intense, emotional, and infuriating. If reading about fatphobia and misogyny in the healthcare system is in any way triggering for you, please proceed with caution and stop if it gets too painful for you.

foreword

They always say the truth is stranger than fiction, and this book is a prime example of that. While the romance and friendships in these pages are fictional, the medical part of Hope's story – every single awful and humiliating thing that she goes through, all the pain and grief and hardship and trauma she faces – is one hundred percent true. In fact, she's been through *so* much more than what I can fit into this story.

How do I know that? Because her story is my story. To be honest, there is a *huge* part of me that's terrified of hitting that "publish" button because putting this much of myself into a character, and especially putting all of my insecurities out there for the world to see, is…uncomfortable, to say the least.

Hope has a condition called lymphedema, which is in very advanced stages and has severely impacted her quality of life. This book explains a little about her disability – which is also *my* disability – but if you'd like to know more, this article from the Mayo Clinic is a great place to find a general overview: **https://bit.ly/MayoLymphedema**.

I also want to mention that while Hope is a plus-sized heroine, this is *far* from a fat-positive story. Hope, like me, struggles with pretty severe body dysmorphia and definitely does *not* love herself. With a medical condition that has literally deformed one of her limbs to the point where she's legally disabled, can barely walk, and sticks out like a sore thumb, it's hard for her to see herself as anything other than the freak with the giant leg. She also faces a lot of fatphobia, both internalized and external, particularly from many of the doctors and nurses who are supposed to be helping her. I said this in the trigger warning, but I'll say it again here. If reading about fatphobia and/or body dysmorphia is triggering for you, please, PLEASE proceed with caution and stop reading if you need to. I would hate for this story to cause anyone pain.

But I'm a firm believer that the best stories are always the ones that come from the heart. And, well, this story has been screaming at me for years, so I figure there's probably a reason for it. Maybe it's because another advanced lymphedema patient out there needs to read this and know that there's hope and light at the end of the tunnel when they find the right care team. Maybe it's because I'm supposed to help shine a light on the way overweight patients – especially women – are treated *far* too often in the medical system. Or maybe it's because there's a doctor or nurse out there who needs to see this so they can help make sure their patients don't have to go through what I've endured. Whatever the case is, I'm pushing through my fear and doing the thing that scares me because I have to believe there's a reason why this story just hasn't left my mind despite my efforts to avoid writing it. And if baring my soul like this touches even one person or can help someone else avoid what I've been through, then it will have been worth it.

Finally, I want to let you know that I did something a little different in this book. Hope's healing journey, much like mine, was heavily influenced by music. In fact, there are a few songs that are so integral to the plot and mood of certain chapters that I can't imagine someone reading this book and *not* understanding the role those songs play in telling this story. So, while my usual ridiculously long playlist can be found at the back of this book just like always, I've also included brief notes at the beginning of a few chapters telling you what songs to listen to if you want to get the full effect.

And on that note, happy reading, and I hope you end up loving Hope, Lennon, and their friends and family as much as I do.

Much love,
Carmen

For Mandie, Brittany, Jenn, and Katey. Without the support and encouragement I got from the four of you – even though some of you have never met each other – this book would have died in chapter four, just like it did all the other times I attempted to write it. Words don't exist to tell you how grateful and lucky I am to call you my chosen family. I love you all, and I can't imagine my life without you. And I really hope the day comes when I get to hug your necks and feed you real Kansas City barbecue!

For Brett, my real-life Lennon. How you're still here after everything I put you through with my lymphedema struggles, I still don't know. But even though our life may not ever be the same as it was when we first met, I know the worst is finally behind us. I love you more than anything, and I don't know what I would do without you and the fuzzy butts. Even when they're assholes.

And for the rock star doctor and occupational therapists who have finally gotten me on the road to my new normal. I might be just one person in a sea of patients, but you took the time to listen and get me the help I needed, and for someone like me, that's a rare thing. Thank you for seeing me as a human being instead of just numbers on a chart. Thank you for giving me hope when my situation seemed hopeless. And thank you for everything you do for your patients with chronic health struggles. Trust me, we notice. And we're so grateful to have found you.

"Find the person who will love you because of your differences and not in spite of them and you have found a lover for life."

— leo buscaglia

one

hope

"**M**otherfucker!" I groaned at the top of my lungs as I opened the door for my best friend. Why the fuck I hadn't just given her a key at this point, I didn't know. I needed to rectify that ASAP.

"Jesus fuck, Hope," April gasped, rushing in and shutting the door behind her so my cats wouldn't get out.

As I turned to get back to the couch – the disgusting, lymphatic fluid-soaked couch – my leg gave out from under me, and I had to brace myself on the back of the furniture to break my fall.

April quickly grabbed my shoulders to steady me, then went and got the walker out of my bedroom so I could use it to hobble back to the automatic reclining couch I'd used my tax money to buy last year…and which was now probably completely ruined. Along with three comforters, every skirt, pair of shorts, and towel I owned, and the damn carpet in this apartment.

I was *never* getting my security deposit back when I moved out of here.

"Damn. I leave you alone for a couple of weeks while I'm working overtime, and you fall apart. How have you been taking care of Syd and Vaughn?" she asked once I'd semi-comfortably settled and reclined myself.

"Automatic…feeders," I panted, then let out a wail of agony as the soaked-through dressing on my deep, gaping open wound just barely scraped against the surface of the leg rest. *"FUCK ME IN THE ASS!"*

"Talk to me, Hope. Tell me what's wrong." April's voice was strained, and I could tell she was trying like hell to keep her nursing training front and center so she wouldn't lose it right along with me.

"It fucking burns! GODDAMN MOTHERFUCKING FUCKER FUCK!"

"Think you've said the word 'fuck' enough times yet?"

I glared at her. "Swearing increases pain tolerance. *MythBusters* proved it."

"Hope, we need to get you to the hospital. Please," she begged. "I'll go with you. I'll talk shop with the doctors and get them to listen. But you have to do something. This amount of pain isn't normal. Not even for you."

"You think I don't know that, April?" I screamed with tears streaming down my face. "But I can't get down the fucking stairs! I can't even stand up!"

"That's what ambulances are for," she said, fumbling through her bag for her phone.

"No," I sobbed. "I can't afford a fucking ambulance! I can't afford to go to the ER."

"Fuck the bill, Hope! Worry about that later. Right now, you need to worry about *you*. You need help, and I'm not strong enough to help you get down the stairs. I'm calling an ambulance," she insisted as she pulled her phone out and dialed the number.

She gave the 911 dispatcher my information and explained my condition and situation much better than I could have in my present state. I guessed that was a perk of having a nurse for a best friend. Then she got my cats, Sydney and Vaughn, into my bedroom and got their food and water feeders and self-cleaning litter box set up in there for them.

April and I had been best friends ever since I'd moved to Portland for college, on the complete opposite side of the country from my family in North Carolina. We'd met at a local coffee shop when I accidentally bumped into her and spilled a huge, full iced latte all over her scrubs, and the rest was history.

When my condition got so bad I could barely leave the apartment and I'd had to go on long-term disability from my job, I'd been convinced I'd lose her friendship. My leg was hideous to look at and had been getting progressively worse for the past two years, and I had been sure no one would ever willingly put themselves in the same room with me. But instead, April had stepped up and been more supportive than any of my family members, who had all told me I needed to lose weight and that was why this was happening. She got my grocery orders for me, helped me take care of the cats when I couldn't do it myself, and usually came by at least a couple of times a week to check up on me, help me at least do a sponge bath if I couldn't handle getting into the shower, and re-dress my open wounds.

She'd called or texted me every day while she was working two straight weeks of overtime shifts at the hospital, and I knew she felt horrible that she was so exhausted she'd just pass out the second her head hit the pillow when she got home. Because I didn't want to make her feel even worse, I'd been downplaying how bad my wounds had gotten. I didn't want her worrying about me when she didn't have the time or energy to come help me.

Until today happened and I just couldn't do it anymore. And one phone call was all it took for April to drop everything, call in to work telling them she had a family emergency, and come help me.

Not even five minutes after she hung up with the emergency dispatcher, there was a knock at the door, and four EMTs came in. One of them walked over to me and knelt in front of me.

If I hadn't been in such excruciating pain, I might have noticed how good-looking this man was. As it was, all I cared about was how humiliated I was that I was twenty-eight years old and had a leg the size of a tree trunk and couldn't stand up.

"How are you doing, ma'am?" he asked.

Ugh. Ma'am? Really? Because that didn't make me feel older than I already did.

I groaned, mostly in pain, but partially in frustration too.

"Sounds like you're in a lot of pain. Can you tell me where your pain is?" the EMT asked.

"My leg," I whimpered. "It feels like someone poured battery acid on my calf."

"How bad is it on a scale of one to ten?"

Of all the damn questions that countless doctors and nurses had asked me over the past five years, this was one of my least favorites. Right up there with asking me if I'd ever considered weight loss surgery. Because the thing was, not only did no one ever seem to care about my answers or believe me when I told them how bad it was, but for someone with chronic pain, the one to ten scale was whacked. I *lived* at somewhere around a four or a five all the time. I was never *not* hurting.

Today, my leg hurt so badly that I couldn't put any weight on it at all. But did it feel like someone was cutting it off without anesthesia? Well, no. But at this point, I would have actually preferred that to the constant acute burning and stabbing sensation I'd had for the past four days. At least then I would have known there was an end in sight.

"Nine and a half?" I tried.

"Can you tell me what happened?"

"I have lymphedema," I sniffled, though that part should

have been obvious because of the size of my leg. "I have open wounds that my friend's been helping me dress here at home, and I think one of them might be infected because it's been weeping so much that it's ruined everything in this apartment and it smells like death. I can't walk. I almost collapsed just moving from the couch to the door to let her in."

"Okay. Can you tell me your name, sweetheart?"

"Hope Morrison," I sighed.

"Is it okay if I call you Hope?"

I nodded. I didn't have the fucking energy for this game of twenty questions, but I knew they were just doing their job.

"Is it okay if I check your vital signs, Hope?"

I nodded again and held out my arm for them to get my blood pressure.

"It's easier on her lower arm," April interjected as the EMT started to wrap the blood pressure cuff around my upper arm, where it was almost impossible for them to ever get a reading.

He moved the cuff to my forearm and got my blood pressure and pulse. Not surprisingly, both were through the roof because I was in so much pain.

"She's a type two diabetic," April told him. "She's on two different kinds of insulin."

"Thank you," an EMT that wasn't the guy working with me said. "Any other medications?"

"Yes. She also has sleep apnea and uses a CPAP machine when she sleeps. Um, give me just a second. She has a list of her meds somewhere," she said, disappearing into my room.

They checked my blood sugar, which was surprisingly low given the amount of stress my body was under. But then again, I'd just taken an insulin shot about an hour ago and I'd barely been able to stomach the few saltines I'd managed to choke down.

"Hope, do you think you can walk out the door with help?" the EMT asked. "We have a chair, so you don't have to go down the stairs, but we're not going to be able to get a stretcher in here."

I shook my head. *Maybe* I could stand up and shuffle a couple of steps if I had someone strong to lean on. But walking? Putting one foot in front of the other? Out of the damn question.

"I told the dispatcher to make sure they had the air mattress," April almost growled as she came back out of my bedroom and handed my medication list to the EMT. "She can't put weight on her leg and she's too big to fit on that chair *because* of her leg."

She wasn't wrong. I wasn't a huge person. Before all of this started, I had been a size eighteen, and, yes, I'd gained a couple of pant sizes since then because I'd gotten a lot more sedentary since my leg had started hurting more. Not that I could actually fit into normal pants these days *because* of my giant, hideous leg. But that goddamn leg, the bane of my existence, tipped me over from just being "obese" to being "morbidly obese."

As April kept talking to the medics and telling them everything they needed to know – because there wasn't a single thing about me and my condition that she didn't know – I kind of checked out of the conversation. I was in too much pain to keep up. I did know that April eventually convinced them to bring the blow-up mattress up. She told them to take me to Kingman Medical Center, where she worked. She knew people there, so she knew she'd be able to make sure I got the treatment I needed, and that was also where my lymphedema therapist and wound care doctor – who hadn't really done a whole lot for me – were based, so at least they'd be able to get my records.

"Okay, Hope, I'm going to help you stand up. You can put all your weight on me if you need to. And then we're going to have to shuffle two steps to the side to get away from the couch so we can slide the air mattress in behind you. All you have to do is sit back down when I tell you to," the medic who had been talking to me the whole time explained.

Somehow, I managed to obey. Then again, I'd powered through this debilitating pain the best I could, using only over-the-counter pain medication because the wound care center didn't believe me anymore when I told them how much pain I was in, for months. What was a few more minutes of agony?

At least I had a medic who was built like a tank here to catch me if I fell.

"My friend's probably out in the waiting room. Can I have my purse so I can call her and tell her what room I'm in?" I asked the nurse in the ER. "She's got my medication list. And she's my authorized liaison."

"Just a minute, honey. Can you tell me what's going on?" the nurse asked.

I groaned. "I told you. I have lymphedema, I have open wounds on my calf that won't heal, and my entire lower leg feels like someone poured battery acid on it. I've had cellulitis in this leg before, so I know what it feels like, and I think I have it again. And something else is wrong too, because this hurts too much to just be because of that."

"Are you having any pain right now?"

"I just told you it feels like someone poured battery acid on it!" I snapped. "Yes, I'm having pain! And before you ask, it's a ten. I can't even think straight because all I can concentrate on is how much it hurts."

"Okay, let me take a look."

The nurse pulled the soggy dressing I'd managed to do a shitty job of applying this morning away from the worst wound – the one that had started turning black – and promptly gagged and ran out of the room with her hand over her mouth.

I wished I could say that I was ashamed or humiliated, or even angry at her, but all I could feel was agony. And pity, because I knew that wound currently smelled like a combination of rotten eggs and three-day-old Kung Pao chicken. If I'd been her, I would have done the same thing.

"Oh, I hear her," I heard April saying. "Thanks, Millie."

Had I been crying that loudly? I hadn't even realized.

"Hey, you," she said with a small smile as she walked into the room. "How are you holding up?"

"It hurts," I sniffled. "And the nurse just ran out of here gagging at the smell."

"I know, sweetie. I'm so sorry you had to see that," she murmured, squeezing my hand.

"I don't blame her," I mumbled. "I don't know how you didn't do that the second you walked into the apartment."

"Because you're my best friend and I love you, and you are more than this disability and this infection. We're going to get the doctor in here and they'll get you something for the pain, okay?"

Just as she said that, a man wearing a doctor's coat walked in. And even in my pain-induced fog, I would have recognized him anywhere. He was April's ex-boyfriend, Lyle, who she'd broken up with about a month ago after finding out that he was sleeping with half the nurses in the hospital.

He blanched when he saw her. "April, what are you doing here? They transferred you out of the E.R. By *your* request."

"Do you see me wearing scrubs, Lyle?" she spat, and if looks could kill, he would have been six feet under. "I'm here as a *liaison* for my *friend*, Hope Morrison. And as a *doctor*, I'm going to trust you to do your job and help her. Hope, are you authorizing me to give medical information to your doctor on your behalf?"

"Yes," I whimpered.

"Okay, *Doctor Garrison*," April said, staring him down like it was a contest. "Hope has advanced stage lymphedema in her right leg, as I'm sure you can see from the difference in the sizes of her legs. She also has three open wounds that I've been helping her dress at home with supplies that our wound care department ordered for her. She's been leaking lymphatic fluid for several weeks, but it seemed to be relatively under control until now. I wasn't able to go visit her in the past couple of weeks because of my work schedule, and she called me today in tears and barely able to get a word out. I'm sure you can smell how bad the infection is, and she's in extreme pain right now and can't bear any weight on her leg. She keeps saying that it feels like someone poured battery acid on it."

"Hope, can you tell me how long this has been going on for?" he asked, turning to me.

"Her lymphedema began showing almost five years ago," she answered for me. "Even though her leg was swelling and nothing else was, her doctors always insisted that it was just her weight, recommended a gastric bypass, and never ran tests or diagnosed it further. She's been on disability for two years, and it's gotten worse, not better. It's been a very long and frustrating road for her, and she needs help."

Lyle nodded, then looked at me. "Hope, I know we've met before under less-than-ideal circumstances, but I swore an oath to help my patients, and I *will* get you the help you need today if you'll let me. Regardless of my history with your friend, you're my patient, not her. But if you'd like a different doctor, that's your right. Are you okay with me treating you today?"

I nodded and sighed. Lyle was an asshole personally, but I did know that he was a damn good doctor. Somehow, it always seemed like the better the doctor was, the bigger an asshole they were. And I just wanted this to be over. Right now, I wouldn't have cared if it was Dr. Kevorkian standing in front of me as long as he could get me some damn morphine or dilaudid.

"Okay," he said, giving me a semi-genuine smile. "What's your pain level right now on a scale of one to ten?"

"Eleven," I sniffled. "I normally don't do this, but *please* get me something for it. *Please.* I can't do this anymore. I can't."

"I'll send the nurse in here with some dilaudid as soon as I can," he promised.

Two

hope

I'd been in this damn hospital for what felt like forever, and after drawing some blood and taking a culture from my wounds, the doctor and nurse had just left me in here. They'd sent in an ultrasound tech to do a scan of my leg to confirm that I didn't have a blood clot, even though I could have saved them the time and myself the money and told them that, but since then, no one had even bothered to check on me. Thank God I didn't have to pee, because I wasn't even sure how I'd accomplish that in my present state.

At least I'd gotten some pain relief while I was waiting. I was almost asleep thanks to the two doses of dilaudid that they'd had to administer to get my pain down to a manageable level. And by manageable, I mean it still hurt like a motherfucker, but I no longer felt like begging someone to just put me out of my misery by sawing my damn leg off with a rusty butter knife.

"You don't have to stay here with me," I mumbled to April for the fourth time. "I'll call and tell you what they say."

"I'm not going *anywhere* until you get admitted," she insisted. "And if they try to send you home in this condition, I'm going to read them the riot act and make them admit you, even if just because you need the pain management."

I let out an exhausted sigh as my eyelids started to flutter closed. I was so tired. Not just physically, but mentally. Emotionally. Spiritually. I'd been fighting this battle with my own body for so long, and I just didn't have the strength left to fight anymore. This was the first time in *weeks* that I'd actually been semi-comfortable enough to relax. I'd been sleeping maybe three hours a night for the past few weeks because of the pain.

I tried to force my eyes back open because I hated the idea of sleeping while April was here keeping me company, but of course, she saw.

"Get some rest, sweetie," she murmured. "I'll wake you up when someone comes in."

But just as she said that, there was a rap on the door, and then Lyle walked back into the room.

"Hi, Hope," he said in a sickly-sweet voice that told me I wasn't going to like whatever came out of his mouth. "How's the pain now?"

"Seven," I slurred slightly.

"I'm glad to hear it's going down. I'm sorry we couldn't do more."

I shrugged. "It's life. At least I don't feel like screaming anymore."

"Well, I got your labs back, and I can see why you're hurting so badly. You've got both a strep infection and a staph infection in that leg. You're flagging for sepsis, so I'm going to get you admitted for some IV antibiotics and fluids so we can try to get it under control. And I'm going to leave a note for the intake physician to put a call in to our wound care team so we can get those wounds taken care of, and hopefully get you started with some lymphedema therapy too."

I nodded, too drained to talk any more.

"Do we have a room number yet?" April asked.

Lyle shook his head. "Sorry. I just put the order in ten minutes ago."

She huffed out an annoyed sigh. "Okay. Thanks, Dr. Garrison."

He gave her a brief nod, then turned back to me. "I hope you get to feeling better soon, Hope."

"Thank you," I garbled.

After he left, the full reality of this situation came crashing down on me.

"What am I going to do about Syd and Vaughn?" I sniffled, swallowing past the ache that had started to build in the back of my throat at the thought that I wouldn't be seeing my sweet fluffballs for God knew how long.

"What kind of friend do you take me for?" April chuckled weakly. "They're going to live with me until you get to go back home, and I'll video chat with you as much as I can so you can still see them. And speaking of you not going home for a little while, what do you want me to bring you from the apartment?"

"Um, my computer. And my iPod," I mumbled. "Maybe I can get some writing done while I'm here."

Ever since I'd gone on disability, I'd started writing romance novels just to give myself something to do. I had a B.A. in English Literature, even though I'd never really had a chance to use it, so I'd taken plenty of creative writing classes. And since being without a job had left me with nothing but time, I'd learned how to make my own covers and do my own formatting, and then I'd self-published my books.

While I wasn't raking in the dough by any stretch of the imagination, I'd built up a small, but loyal fan base who were always chomping at the bit for the next story. I was currently working on my sixth book, which was sort of a fanfiction about one of my favorite TV shows, *Alias*. Except without the stupid parts, and with enough changed that it wasn't copyright infringement. I was absolutely loving Kellan and Meadow's story, and I couldn't wait to share it with my readers.

April gave me a sad smile. "I know your books are your happy place, but don't beat yourself up if you don't have the energy to work on them. *You* need to be your first priority right now. Your readers can wait. And I'm sure if you tell them you're in the hospital, they'll tell you the same thing."

"I know. But if nothing else, I can binge *Alias* and *Criminal Minds*. I'm *not* staying in here without some kind of decent entertainment."

That earned me a snort. "Fair. Hey, did you message your friend Peyton to let her know what's going on?"

I shook my head. "Didn't have a chance."

She dug through my purse until she found my cellphone and handed it to me. "If I know you at all, you're not going to make a post in your reader group, but you should at least tell her. You know she'll want to know."

I managed half a smile, despite the pain and bone-deep exhaustion.

Peyton was so much more than just one of my readers. We'd met in a Facebook group for romance book lovers around the time I'd stopped working and had immediately bonded over our mutual love of happily-ever-afters. Now she was my alpha reader – reading my books as I wrote them to make sure they didn't suck – my proofreader, and also did some virtual assistant tasks for me occasionally. But what had started as a friendship born of mutual interests had quickly developed into so much more. We were more like sisters who lived on opposite ends of the country.

Unfortunately, while she loved reading about happy endings in books, she'd all but lost faith in ever finding her own. She'd gotten married to a police officer from her church when she was twenty, but it turned out that a vicious monster had been lurking underneath the charming exterior he showed the public.

He'd snowed everyone in their lives, including her parents, into believing he was the most wonderful man on the planet, leaving her with nowhere to go and no one to turn to...provided she could ever find the courage to leave at all.

I didn't even know what Peyton looked like or what her last name was because the Facebook profile I knew was a fake profile she'd made using a burner cellphone she'd bought with spare grocery money she'd saved up. She'd used the last name of one of her favorite characters from a romance novel, and her profile picture was a famous quote from *Pride and Prejudice*.

Some people might have said I was being reckless sharing so much of my personal life with someone I'd never even seen a picture of and just believing the things she told me about her life without question, but somehow, I just *knew* I could trust her. Just like she knew she could trust me with everything she'd told me about her life. And we *had* talked on the phone via Facebook Messenger a few times.

That was why I knew she'd want to know I'd finally caved and gone to the E.R. today. She'd been trying to get me to come to the hospital for the past week, but because I hadn't thought anyone would take me seriously, I'd refused until today.

Unlocking my phone, I quickly navigated to our message thread and was pleasantly surprised to see that she was online.

ME

> So...I caved. I told April how bad that one wound was and she called in to work so she could come to the hospital with me. Prognosis is a staph and strep infection, and they said I was flagging for sepsis, so they're admitting me for IV antibiotics. I'm just waiting for them to find a room for me.

PEYTON

Flagging for sepsis??? Not good!

ME

They had to give me 2 doses of dilaudid to even begin to touch my pain. I'm still at like a 7, but at least I'm loopy enough that I don't care anymore. 🤪

PEYTON

I hate to say I'm glad you're there because I know this sucks, but you're where you need to be right now. Hopefully your doctor can get you the help you need.

ME

I kid you not, my E.R. doc was April's ex. AWKWARD!

PEYTON

Ryan Gosling chuckling GIF

You should make a romcom out of that. After you finish Kellan and Meadow, because I NEEEEEEED the rest of their story!

ME

Woman, you know I don't do romcoms.

> I need my glass of salty tears!

> *Anjelica Houston sipping tea GIF*

PEYTON

> Fair. I mean, maybe a romcom with feels?

ME

> Sure, I'll go ahead and add that to the zillion other stories you've convinced me to write. 😛

A knock on the door interrupted our conversation, and I looked up just as two techs came into the room.

"Hi. Hope?" one of them asked.

I nodded.

"I'm Jacob, and this is Ben. We're going to take you up to your room, okay?"

"Okay," I sighed. "Thanks."

"Hope, are you going to be okay if I go get the cats situated at my place and get a bag packed for you?" April asked as she put my purse next to me on the bed.

I nodded. "Thanks. I'm sure they're going to want me to change into a gown, but can you grab me some clothes just in case? If I have any clean ones."

"Of course. Anything else besides your computer, iPod, and chargers?"

"No," I mumbled. "Oh, wait. My CPAP."

"Oh, duh!" She smacked her forehead. "Good thing you remembered that, because I completely forgot."

"And make yourself a copy of my key while you're at it. I don't know why I didn't do that a long time ago."

April chuckled. "Okay."

"We're taking her to room 247," one of the techs told her. "Visiting hours end at eight, so you've got plenty of time."

"Okay, thanks," she said. "I'll be back as soon as I can, Hope."

"Can I help you?" came the disembodied voice through my call button.

"I have to use the bathroom," I sniffled as my stomach started to twist into a knot.

"Okay, I'll send someone in."

I honestly had no idea how I was going to manage this. Peeing was something that most people just took for granted. They didn't have to think about how they were going to accomplish it. It was just muscle memory: get out of bed, walk to the toilet, do your business, wash your hands, and get back to bed.

But for me, right now? I had to think about every single aspect of that in excruciating detail. This bed was at least a foot higher than my bed at home, which meant I couldn't get both feet flat on the ground before I stood up. That meant I'd be sliding down the side of the bed…onto my bad leg, because all of the equipment that was hooked up to me was on the other side. At least they'd brought a commode into the room, so if I managed to get up, I'd only have about six steps to walk to the plastic shower chair with a bucket under it.

And to add insult to injury, the dilaudid they'd administered in the E.R. had started to wear off, and all the physician who had written up my admittance paperwork had allowed me to have for pain was one Norco, which was doing absolutely nothing. Which meant I was back to the battery acid and white-hot branding iron stabbing pain from this morning. I honestly wasn't sure if I would even be able to stand up, but I hated the thought of a bedpan, so I knew I had to try.

A light rap sounded on the door, and the middle-aged nurse with the worst case of resting bitch face I'd ever seen – who had briefly introduced herself to me as Linda when I'd been brought up here two hours ago – walked in, accompanied by a male tech who was built like a twig. My orders stated that I needed to be assisted by two people if I got out of bed since I was a fall risk, but I guessed they'd failed to specify that said two people needed to be strong enough to…I don't know, actually *help* me get out of bed.

"You need to go to the bathroom?" Linda asked in a bored monotone.

I nodded and started to raise my bed into a sitting position so I'd just have to turn sideways. But because wound care hadn't been up to see me yet, they'd just thrown some chuck pads on the bed and over my leg, so there was no barrier between my wounds and the bed. My leg started to scrape against the coarse cotton on the pads as I raised myself up, and I bit my lip to keep from crying out. If I hadn't known better, I would have sworn someone had slipped a cheese grater underneath me when I wasn't looking.

Once I was sitting up, I started to turn sideways, and there was no holding it in anymore. A groan of agony escaped me as my leg hit the siderail of the bed right on the worst of my wounds. The pain was so intense and all-consuming that it felt like it was permeating every fiber of my being, and I had to swallow down the bile that rose in my throat to keep myself from losing the disgusting lunch/dinner they'd brought me an hour ago.

"Can you stand up?" Linda huffed.

I nodded. "Just…give me…a—"

"How are you doing this at home?" she bit out.

"I—" I choked out, then hissed as I tried to move my leg again and managed to get it maybe half an inch further out of bed.

"How are you doing this at home?" she snapped again.

"My…bed—"

"How. Are. You. Doing. This. At. Home?!" she cut me off, yelling at me like I was a senile old lady.

A sob started to work its way up my throat, but I swallowed it down. Crying wouldn't help me get through this simple task that felt tantamount to climbing Mount Everest right now. And if I wanted to get a word in edgewise to explain to this woman that my bed at home was a lot closer to the floor – and that I couldn't actually remember the last time I'd been able to get my damn leg up into bed at all and I slept with it hanging down on the floor – I couldn't start crying. Once I finally gave in to the tears, I knew it would take a damn long time for them to stop.

"My bed is—"

"No, I'm not doing this," she practically growled. "Get back in bed. We're getting a bedpan."

That made another sob start to build up, and this time I couldn't help the whimper that came out. She just huffed out an annoyed sigh and stomped out of the room like a five-year-old having a temper tantrum, while the tech, whose name I didn't even know, just stood there like a deer in headlights.

Linda was back in less than five minutes with a bedpan that looked like it was made for a small child. There was no way in hell that I'd ever be able to get on that thing correctly.

"Roll onto your side," she barked.

With every last bit of strength I possessed, I grabbed the handrail on my right side and pulled myself halfway onto my side, lifting my left hip as much as possible. But as my leg scraped against the soaked-through chuck pad, I cried out in pain.

"Gah!" I wailed. "I...can't...stay... Put it down. Please."

"Roll over more. I can't fit this under you," Linda snarled.

"I...I can't," I whimpered. "Please...I can't. It hurts too much."

"Whatever," she muttered, shoving the bedpan halfway under me. "Just go."

I rolled back onto my back and tried to use my good leg to shift myself a little further onto the bedpan, but by this point, I had to pee so bad that I had no choice but to let it happen...all over the damn bed. Maybe a quarter of it actually made it into the bedpan.

"Josh, go get new sheets so we can do a bed change," Linda ordered, letting out an annoyed sigh, then turned back to me with a scowl. "You're going to have to figure something out. We can't keep changing your bed every time we do this."

Didn't she think I knew that? I wasn't an idiot. But right now, I was in so much pain I couldn't even think straight. So whatever the solution was, I couldn't come up with it. Except for one, which I had a feeling they'd say no to.

"Can I get a catheter?" I asked. "My leg is too big and it hurts too much for me to roll over enough to get the bedpan under me. Maybe in a day or two, it'll be better, but I just can't right now."

"I'll ask the doctor, but they usually won't do catheters for patients who are ambulatory," she grumbled.

But I'm not *ambulatory right now! Can't you see that?!* I wanted to scream.

"Okay," was what came out instead.

Thankfully, Josh came back into the room right then, and after a *lot* of pain and wails of agony, they were able to get my bed changed.

Then they left, closing the door behind them. And now that I was finally alone, I let it all out. I cried and cried and cried until the sobs wracked my body and I could barely breathe.

I'd come here because I needed help, but just like every other health care professional who'd ever seen me for my lymphedema, this nurse had taken one look at me and just written me off as a melodramatic, drug-seeking, morbidly obese waste of space. I guessed it was nice to know some things never changed.

Three

lennon

Tonight was going to suck. Bad. This hall was completely full. Not one single empty room. And one of our nurses had a family emergency, so it was just me and my friend Brady working the overnight shift on this hall, with the help of a few techs.

Granted, the overnight shift was usually a little quieter than the day shift, which was why I liked it, but there was still plenty to do, especially with a full house. We'd be lucky if we got lunch breaks.

I was cursing my luck getting a bunch of men my grandfather's age – who were notoriously easily agitated – when Linda, the day nurse I was taking over for, led me and my tech for the evening, Tanisha, into the last room for the handoff.

I heard whimpering and sniffling coming from the room before we even walked in, and I could immediately tell it wasn't an old man.

"This is Hope Morrison," Linda started. "She was just admitted this afternoon. Twenty-eight-year-old female, presented with severe lymphedema in right lower extremity. Open wounds with an odorous discharge, complaining of severe burning pain in her calf. Cultures revealed both staph and strep infections, and she flagged for sepsis. IV Cefazolin and Vancomycin have been prescribed, along with IV Diflucan for a possible yeast infection in one of the folds of her leg. Type two diabetic, on Novolog insulin with meals and Lantus overnight. ADA diet. Also on levothyroxine, low dose aspirin, and ferrous sulfate. Norco has been prescribed for pain as needed. She can't bear weight on her leg. Attempted to get her up to go to the commode, but she wasn't able to stand."

I saw the patient visibly bristle when Linda mentioned the commode, and something told me there was more to that story. Linda could be…impatient, I guessed. And also judgmental at times. She tended to just see the numbers on the chart and base her entire opinion of the person she was caring for on said numbers. This wouldn't have been the first time, or even the second or third time, someone had an issue with her.

"She's on a bedpan for now," she continued. "However, she has asked for a catheter due to the size of her leg and her not being able to lie on the bedpan correctly. I haven't heard back from the doctor about that yet."

I nodded as I tried to process the information that had just been fired at me at a mile a minute. And it was only then that I really looked at the woman lying on the bed in front of me.

My heart squeezed as I saw the agony on her face. The expression that told me she'd been conditioned, over years, to just grin and bear the pain she was in because no one had taken her seriously – and that she was currently in worse pain than I'd ever felt in my entire life. I'd gotten pretty good at being able to tell when someone was faking pain to try to get medication, and this was one hundred percent genuine.

Being a nurse, I tried my best to view patients clinically. Not to get too personally involved. If I let myself feel everything for every patient who came through these doors, I'd have been leaving in tears every day. But there was no viewing this woman clinically.

Underneath the puffy red eyes and sweaty forehead was one of the most beautiful women I'd ever seen. Her bright red hair splayed in a mess across the pillow, and her beautiful hazel eyes that were brimming over with tears drew me in, beckoning me to discover the soul behind them.

"Hi, Miss Morrison," I said quietly, afraid to speak any louder and let my voice betray how much sympathy I already had for this poor woman.

"You can call me Hope," she sniffled.

Even while she was crying, her voice was as beautiful as she was. Though I couldn't help thinking about the irony of her name. I could tell she hadn't had any hope in a long time.

I smiled. "Hi, Hope. I'm Lennon, and I'm going to be taking care of you tonight. And this is Tanisha, my tech. She's going to be helping me out."

"Nice to meet you guys. I wish it was under better circumstances," Hope chuckled, sniffling again, but cracking a small smile.

This girl was a trooper. She was obviously in excruciating pain, but she was still smiling and even attempting to laugh.

"Hope, did you get a chance to have dinner yet?" I asked.

"Sort of? By the time the lunch I ordered got up here, it was already dinnertime according to the kitchen, so I had a super late lunch at four-thirty."

"Okay. I'll see if I can get you a box lunch to take your meds with tonight."

"Thanks. I appreciate it," Hope sighed.

"Is there anything else I can do for you right now?"

"Um, do you know when I'm allowed to have my next dose of pain meds?" she said in a small voice, like she was afraid to even ask for relief from the agony she was in.

Linda looked at her chart for a moment, checking when she'd last administered a dose. "She can have more Norco at nine."

I saw Hope swallow hard and squeeze her eyes shut, like she was trying not to cry at the fact that she wasn't allowed to have another dose of pain meds for almost two hours.

God, this poor girl. What doctor had set up her pain management protocol? It obviously wasn't even making a dent in her misery.

"Okay, thanks," she mumbled, accenting it with a soft sniffle.

While Tanisha started to get a set of vitals, I left and went to hunt down one of the premade box lunches to take back to Hope. I needed to talk to her and get some more information about her condition so I could try to get the on-call doctor to authorize something stronger than Norco at least for tonight so she could get some sleep, which I could tell she sorely needed.

"Why the fuck doesn't the kitchen stay open past seven?" I heard Brady muttering from next to me. "Sending us scrambling around for food for patients because they were admitted at four is ridiculous."

I chuckled. "You too?"

"Yeah, although I'm not sure if this dude actually missed dinner or just wants a snack," he muttered.

"Have a little compassion, Brady," I bit out. "The guy's in the hospital. So what if he wants a sandwich? Let him have a sandwich."

"Who pissed in your Wheaties, man? Jeez."

"Whoever the goddamn doctor is who put in the pain management protocol for one of my patients," I grumbled. "Just one look at her face tells me she's in a ton of pain, but they've got her on one Norco and she's in tears. Do you know who's on call tonight? I haven't even had a chance to look."

"Youngblood."

Good. Dr. Youngblood was a younger doctor, and she was reasonable. If I presented a convincing case to her, I could probably get her to authorize something stronger for Hope.

"Thanks, man," I said. "See you later."

"Later, Len," he called over his shoulder as he turned around.

I rolled my eyes. Everyone knew I *hated* to be called Len or Lenny. I was named after one of the greatest musicians of all time, and I was proud of it…even though I was half-convinced that my parents had just named me Lennon to be funny because our last name was McCartney.

I could hear Hope from two doors down as I was heading back to her room. Now the whimpers and sniffling from earlier had turned into full-on sobs that made my heart feel like it was ripping in two.

I didn't know why I cared so much. I cared about all of my patients, and if I'd heard any of them crying, of course I'd have tried to find out what the problem was and see if I could help. But hearing one of my patients crying didn't usually make *me* want to cry too.

Maybe it was because I could tell how long Hope had been conditioned to think that her pain didn't matter. Maybe it was because she was my age, which was rare on this floor.

Or maybe it was because I was attracted to her, even like this.

Wait, what?! Hold the damn phone.

That wasn't possible. It had only been eleven months since the accident. Since Candace had been ripped away from me in the blink of an eye and my world had been turned upside-down. There was no way I could even *think* about looking at another woman yet.

Right?

Except that I couldn't deny the instant pull I'd felt to Hope the moment I'd laid eyes on her. What exactly it meant, I didn't know, but I couldn't have ignored it if I tried.

Not that I'd ever have done anything about it. I liked my job too much to even think about crossing that line.

When I walked into room 247, Hope had tears streaming

down her face and seemed like she was struggling to catch a breath. I tried my best to smile as I pulled one of the chairs in the room over to sit down next to her bed. I had my hospital-issued phone and smart watch, so I'd know if someone else needed me, but right now, she clearly did.

"Hey," I said quietly, handing her the box lunch. "I managed to find a sandwich and chips for you."

"Thanks," she sniffled.

"Want to talk about it?"

"About what? My sandwich?"

I let out a quiet snort. "No, about whatever has you in tears right now."

Apparently that was the wrong thing to say, because that made the crying even worse. Even though it was technically crossing a line, I couldn't stop myself from reaching for her hand and taking it in both of mine, squeezing gently.

And there it was again. That pull. This time accompanied by a flood of warmth making its way through my whole body at the simple contact.

"I know you don't know me, but if you need to talk, I'm here to listen," I told her. "About anything."

"Don't you have other patients to take care of?" she asked, accenting the question with a hiccup.

I grabbed her water mug and handed it to her. She took it from me and took a sip, then started looking around, like she couldn't find something.

"What do you need?" I asked.

"I can't find the bed controls. I need to sit up if I'm going to eat this sandwich," she sniffled.

I found her all-in-one remote and handed it to her, and she raised the bed up, hissing and groaning as she did. Yep, it was at least partially the pain that had her in tears.

"Your leg's hurting pretty bad, huh?"

She nodded, and more tears filled her eyes. "It took two doses of dilaudid to get me down from an eleven to a seven in the E.R., and now they're giving me Norco. I don't want to sound like I'm just looking for pain meds, but what exactly do they think that's going to do for my pain when it took *two* doses of the strongest thing you have to get it under control before?"

Two doses of dilaudid? And the internist in charge of her case had put her on Norco? Who the fuck had come up with that bright idea?

I looked at the dry erase board on the wall that had her basic information on it and rolled my eyes when I saw the name. Dr. Upton was a grade-A alpha male douchebag who always thought women were exaggerating their pain. He should have retired ten years ago, but his misogynistic ass was still here making women's lives – and sometimes men's lives – miserable on a daily basis.

"And then a couple of hours after I got admitted, I had to pee, and that nurse, Linda, was in here with one of the techs," Hope continued before I could ask anything else. "I was moving super slow because just moving my leg makes it hurt so bad I want to scream, and I was struggling because this bed is at least a foot higher than my bed at home. But she just kept going, 'How are you doing this at home? How are you doing this at home? *How are you doing this at home*?' over and over and over again. Like, she was literally yelling at me and talking to me like I was slow. Sh-she didn't even give me a chance to…to get a word in."

New tears welled up as she was talking, and she took a deep breath as she scrubbed them away with the back of her hand. I could tell she was right on the edge of a complete meltdown, and the urge to pull her into my arms, hold her tight, and promise her that everything would get better was overwhelming.

I didn't understand why I felt this way. There wasn't a single rational explanation for it. But I couldn't deny it if I tried.

And I also couldn't do that. I shouldn't have even been holding her hand. Besides, what she really wanted – the one thing that could make any of this better for her – was the one thing I couldn't give her. At least not until I talked to Dr. Youngblood.

"Linda finally just snapped at me and told me she wasn't going to deal with getting me out of bed and that she was getting a bedpan," she went on. "And when I pissed all over the bed because I couldn't get all the way on the bedpan, she got all snippy about that too because they had to clean me up and do a bed change. When I asked about the catheter, she snapped at me and said that doctors usually won't do them for patients who are ambulatory. But I'm *not* ambulatory right now. I hate the idea of a catheter, but I hate the idea of pissing all over the bed every time I have to pee more, so I don't know what else to do."

My blood was boiling by the time she was done talking. I wished I'd been here and seen that so I could have reported Linda to her supervisor. Yelling at a patient and belittling them was *never* okay, and neither was getting upset at them for something they couldn't control, like not being able to lie on the bedpan properly. But I hadn't seen it, so I couldn't say anything. I *could,* however, tell Hope how to make sure Linda was never assigned to her again.

"Shit, I'm sorry," Hope muttered with another sniffle as she swiped at her eyes again. "You didn't need to hear that."

"Sure, I did. I told you, I'm here to listen," I assured her. "Look, tomorrow morning, you need to ask to talk to a patient advocate. Tell them what you just told me about Linda. You don't deserve to be treated that way, and you don't have to stand for it. They can make sure it's documented, and they can also make sure she doesn't have anything to do with your case anymore."

Her eyes went wide, like this was the first time she'd ever heard that she could advocate for herself if she wasn't being treated with respect and dignity.

"Really?"

I gave her a sad half-smile. "Yes, really. The doctors, nurses, techs...we're all supposed to be helping you. If you don't feel like you're being respected, the hospital needs to know about it. Now, do you mind if I take a look at your leg?"

"I...I guess. Just please be careful around my calf," she said hesitantly. "It hurts so bad."

"I will," I promised.

As soon as I lifted the blanket and sheet off of Hope's legs, I had to stop myself from gasping out loud. Her right leg was more than twice the size of her left, from her foot all the way up to her hip. She had three different open wounds that just had our chuck pads thrown over them rather than having proper dressings put on them. And even though I'd encountered some *rank* odors working here, I'd never smelled anything like the discharge coming out of her leg right now, which was from a wound that was at least five or six centimeters deep and was actually turning black, like the tissue had started to die. Why wouldn't someone have packed and dressed this?

And then there was the size difference in her legs. How in the hell had any doctor allowed this obvious case of lymphedema to get this bad? Whoever her doctor was, they needed to lose their license over this shit. Her leg literally looked like something you'd see on one of those reality shows for weird diseases.

"They didn't dress your wounds?" I asked, wanting the answer to the most pressing of my *many* questions first.

Hope shook her head. "No. The doctor said he wanted wound care to look at them first, but they never came."

"Is it okay if I get some supplies to dress it? Just so it's not left open overnight. They'll still be able to get it off tomorrow."

"Please don't," she whimpered. "It hurts too much. They just have the chucks on the bed so I won't drain onto the sheets."

"What kind of pain is it?" I pressed. "Aching, burning, stabbing?"

"It feels like someone poured battery acid on my calf," she sobbed. "It burns so much. And the wounds… Any time I move my leg, it feels like I'm running it over a cheese grater."

"I know you probably hate this question, but—"

"Eight," she cut me off, telling me where she was at on the pain scale.

"It's like you're reading my mind," I teased. "Look, I'm not going to make any promises, but I'm going to talk to the doctor on call and see if there's anything more I can do for you. Okay?"

Cue another round of sobs. I opened the untouched box of tissues on her tray table and handed them to her. She grabbed one and dabbed at her eyes with it.

"Sorry," she sniffled.

"Don't be sorry. No one likes being in the hospital, especially when they're in pain. Is there *anything* I can do to make you more comfortable right now?"

"Not unless you want to slip me some morphine or dilaudid and not tell anyone." She sighed. "Or bring my cats here. I know it's stupid, but I miss them."

I smiled. "It's not stupid at all. How many cats do you have?"

I knew what she really wanted and needed was pain relief, but if I could get her to focus on something else for a little bit, maybe it would take her mind off the pain while I tried to get a hold of Dr. Youngblood.

"Two," she sniffled, grabbing her phone and turning it on before turning the screen toward me.

I found myself looking at one all-black cat and another all-white one. I wasn't a cat person by any stretch of the imagination, but I had to admit they were cute.

"Are their names Yin and Yang?" I teased.

She giggled through her tears. And God, I loved that sound. More than I could explain. Maybe because it was such a relief to hear something that wasn't a sob coming out of her.

"No. The white one is Sydney and the black one is Vaughn."

"Sydney and Vaughn? Like the *Alias* characters?"

Her face lit up in the first real smile I'd seen all night, and my heart almost burst. She had the most beautiful smile. I hated that it was being suppressed by her pain right now.

And why the hell was I even thinking about how beautiful her smile was?

"Yeah. *Alias* is one of my favorite shows."

"It's my guilty pleasure show," I admitted. "I never got into

Lost, though."

"The only good thing about *Lost* was Ian Somerhalder," she giggled. "And the Greg Grunberg cameo in the pilot episode."

I chuckled. And then the phone and smart watch went off, telling me another patient was calling me.

"Look, I have to go check on another patient. But right after that, I'm going to try to get in touch with our on-call doctor. I'll be back a little later to give you your nighttime meds, and I'll let you know what I find out about your pain management protocol. Okay?"

"I'm not holding my breath," she sighed. "But thank you. For caring."

What kind of hell had this girl been through that she was actually thanking me for caring about her?

"You're welcome. For the sandwich," I said with a wink.

She giggled again, and I decided that my goal tonight was going to be to keep her laughing if I couldn't get her pain under control enough for her to get some sleep. Because it would keep her mind off the pain, but also because her laugh just might have been my new favorite sound.

four

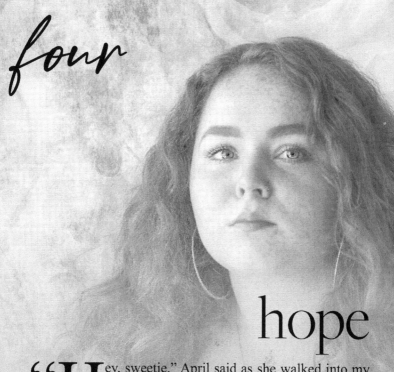

hope

"**H**ey, sweetie," April said as she walked into my room. "Sorry I was gone for so long."

"You're helping me," I sighed. "Don't apologize. Are the kitties okay?"

She smiled. "A little freaked out, but they'll be fine. Anyway, I come bearing entertainment. I have your laptop, your iPod, and all of your charging cords. And I brought your CPAP machine, your memory foam pillow, and a clean comforter too. I know our pillows and blankets here suck."

"Thanks," I sniffled. "Why the hell did the stupid internist only put me on Norco? It took *two* doses of dilaudid to get my pain down to a manageable level. What does he think one Norco is going to do?"

"You need to ask to talk to a patient advocate in the morning. They can get a different internist assigned to your case. But unfortunately, unless you get a nurse who's willing to talk to the on-call doctor tonight, you're going to be in for a rough night," she sighed as she got my pillow under my head and draped the comforter over the hospital blankets, then pulled my CPAP machine out of its case and started to get it hooked up.

"My nurse actually said he was going to. Whether or not he does remains to be seen. And he also told me to talk to the patient advocate. The nurse who was here when I first got into the room literally yelled at me when I took too long to get out of bed to pee, and when I told him about that, he said I needed to report it."

Lennon had seemed so sweet and genuine. And he hadn't seemed like he was grossed out looking at my leg, like so many doctors and nurses had before. But I knew he was probably just as disgusted by me as everyone else was. He was just able to hide it better.

If only I could have reminded myself of that so I wouldn't develop a crush on the guy who was going to have to change my sheets if I had to use the bedpan tonight. Oh, and who was going to have to wipe me when I did.

God, this was humiliating. Of course my nurse tonight had to be a guy my age with the body of a freaking Greek god. He was seriously gorgeous. Tall and lean, but still buff and strong, with short light brown hair and gorgeous brown eyes. And his smile. Swoon!

"Who's your nurse tonight?" April's voice pulled me out of my daydream.

"Lennon."

"Good. If he said he's going to talk to the on-call doctor, he's going to talk to them. He's one of the good ones, and a total sweetheart. Plus, he's fun to look at," she chuckled, putting my CPAP mask on the bed next to me where I could reach it.

"Right?" I agreed. "Of course my nurse has to be the world's hottest guy. Because having him have to wipe my ass for me isn't at all embarrassing."

"Thanks for the compliment," came Lennon's voice from the other side of the room. "I'll try not to let it go to my head."

I groaned and felt myself blush crimson. Add that to the list of reasons why this was the most mortifying and awful day ever.

"Hey, April," he said. "I'm guessing this was your family emergency?"

"Yep. Hope's my sister from another mister, and she doesn't have any family here, so I'm her emergency contact. I'm gonna have to talk to Adam tomorrow morning and get him to put me on another floor while she's here. Take good care of her for me, okay?"

"I promise she's in good hands tonight," Lennon said with a smile, then looked back at me. "And Hope, as for the other thing you just said, you're not the first person I've had to help like that, nor will you be the last. You have no reason to be humiliated because you need a little extra help right now. That's my job, and I'm happy to do it. And trust me when I say there's not much I haven't seen."

"Except a leg like mine, I'm sure," I said.

"Okay, you got me there," he chuckled. "I guess you *are* my first in that respect."

"Don't worry, I'll be gentle," I teased.

Lennon and April both laughed.

I was surprised at my ability to make a joke like that right now, especially considering that he'd just caught me telling April how hot I thought he was. Perks of being a romance author, I guessed. If this was one of my books, that lame joke would probably have been the start of a beautiful love story.

But it wasn't one of my books. It was the real world, and in the real world, guys like him didn't want girls like me. They didn't even give us a second glance. He probably had some gorgeous supermodel-looking wife or girlfriend waiting for him at home. Maybe even a kid or two.

"How long has it been like that?" he asked, flashing that gorgeous smile again.

"It's been getting worse over the past couple of years," I sighed. "But multiple doctors have always just told me it was my weight and I needed weight loss surgery and would scold me when I kept gaining weight despite trying every diet known to man, and despite the fact that all the weight I was gaining was in my leg. I kept begging them to do tests and help me, but they never would.

"When I started getting wounds, I went to the wound care center on my own because I knew my doctor wouldn't do anything about it. April told me there was no reason to pay them to do my dressings when she could come by my apartment and do them for free, especially since I can't drive and had to pay for medical transports. And they weren't doing compression or anything else because I'm waiting to go to a vascular consult to see if there's a problem with blood flow in my leg. So, I stopped going, and I've been managing the pain by taking over-the-counter pain meds by the fistful because the wound care center never believed that I was in any real pain. They kept saying it shouldn't hurt that much and told me to take ibuprofen. And now I can barely walk. I've been off work for *years* dealing with this, and it's not getting any better. Ugh. Sorry. I'm rambling. I tend to do that when I talk about this because it's just so frustrating."

"Ramble away," he told me. "It's okay. I'm sorry you've been going through all that."

I shrugged. "It's life. What can I do?"

"Hopefully what you can do is get the help you need here and get better. Anyway, I actually come bearing good news. I got in touch with our on-call doctor, and she's putting in an order for some dilaudid to get you through the night. She's also going to get your case reassigned and make a note for the new doctor to reassess your pain management protocol in the morning. I'm just waiting for the order to go through the pharmacy so I can bring it in to you."

I couldn't help it. I started crying again, this time in relief. Someone cared. Someone was listening to me and believed me when I said how much pain I was in. And he'd actually gone out of his way to talk to a doctor about getting me better pain meds to get through the night.

"Thank you," I sobbed. "Thank you so much."

"Of course. I hate seeing my patients suffering," he said awkwardly, looking down like he was somehow embarrassed about that. "I'll be back with the good drugs and your nighttime meds soon, okay?"

"Thanks," I sniffled.

"Do you need anything else right now?"

"No, I'm good. Thanks." I attempted a smile, but I wasn't entirely successful.

"Actually, she needs some distilled water for her CPAP machine," April interjected. "I got it all set up for her, though."

He nodded. "You've got it. I'll grab some before I come back with your meds."

Lennon left, and I turned back to April, who smiled at me.

"Told you he was one of the good ones."

"Yeah, I guess anyone who likes *Alias* is okay by me," I sighed, cracking half a smile.

"Oh, my God. You've known the guy for all of...what, an hour? And you're already talking about *Alias* with him?" she laughed. "You're obsessed."

"To be fair, he's the one who brought it up. I just told him the cats' names because I said I missed them and he asked about them," I chuckled.

"So he's as big of a dork as you are?"

"I guess. I don't know."

"Look, sweetie, I'm so sorry I can't stay longer, but I have to get some sleep so I can work the overnight shift tomorrow," she said apologetically. "I'll come check on you before I clock in, okay?"

"Don't be sorry. Go get some rest," I told her. "And give the kitties extra snuggles from me."

"Of course I will." She gave me a sad smile. "I know this

sucks, Hope, but maybe it's a blessing in disguise. Maybe this is going to be what finally gets things moving in the right direction."

"I hope so," I sighed. "I need this to be over. I can't keep living like this anymore."

"I know. Do you want me to stay until Lennon gets back with your meds?"

"No, it's okay. I'll just hang out with the original Sydney and Vaughn until he gets back," I chuckled. "Can you maybe just plug my computer and my phone charger in for me?"

"Absolutely."

After April got me situated and gave me a hug goodbye, I pulled *Alias* up on a streaming service and started playing one of my favorite episodes: the first episode of the fourth season. I did the best I could to tune out the pain and just focus on the show, but it didn't do much to make this bearable. I was still in agony, and the feeling of my skin eroding from the acidic lymphatic fluid was back in full force. But I knew if I focused on wondering when Lennon would be back with the dilaudid, it would just make it worse.

"I come bearing gifts," Lennon announced, startling me away from my show.

"Oh, my God!" I exclaimed, jumping in the bed and instantly regretting it when my leg scraped against the chuck pad. "Motherfucker!"

"Is that any way to talk to the guy who has your pain meds?"

I felt myself blush again, though I didn't know why. It wasn't like I was ashamed of talking like a sailor. I'd gotten over that a long time ago.

"Sorry," I mumbled as I hit pause. "My leg's the motherfucker, not you."

"Had a feeling," he chuckled. "Sorry I scared you. Let me scan your wristband so I can give you your nighttime meds. And the goods."

I held my arm out for him to scan the oh-so-stylish bracelet they'd given me when I was admitted. He scanned it and then handed me a little cup full of my pills for the night, which I swallowed in one gulp. After taking fistfuls of over-the-counter pain meds at a time, I'd gotten good at swallowing a ton of pills at once.

"Do you want to do your own insulin shot or do you want me to do it?" he asked me.

I raised my bed up a little straighter. I was a diabetic who hated needles – which worked out *really* well for me – so I liked to do my own shots. I liked controlling when and where the needle would poke me. Most nurses just started to do it themselves without asking, so I appreciated him asking more than he'd ever know.

"Let me do it, please."

"Yeah, of course. Here's your seventy units of Lantus." He handed me the full syringe and an alcohol swab.

I sighed and took my stupid insulin shot. Diabetes could go suck a dick. I hated this stupid disease so fucking much. The disease that had made me overcome my very real fear of needles and that made me poke myself to draw blood multiple times a day.

"Okay, now I've got what you really wanted. Here's your dilaudid," Lennon said as he walked around to my other side, where the IV port was in my arm, and administered the drug. "What do you think about letting me dress your leg once this starts taking effect and you're not hurting as much? I really hate leaving it open and exposed like that. I have no idea why someone didn't dress it after they found out wound care wasn't coming today."

I sighed again. I knew he was doing his job, but I just wanted to let this dilaudid take effect and then try to get some sleep before it wore off. At the same time, though, maybe it wouldn't hurt so bad if it was properly dressed.

"Okay," I conceded.

He smiled. "Okay. I'm going to go grab some supplies. And

the distilled water, because I forgot it. Do you know what April was using at home?"

"Um, Silvercel on the open wounds, and then abdominal pads and those long gauze wraps around the outside. I forget what they're called. And then she'll put a Tubigrip on it to hold everything in place."

"Sounds good. Hang tight. I'll be back soon."

He turned and left me alone again, so I resumed watching my favorite show.

Lennon was back within ten minutes, and I paused the show again. It just felt rude to keep watching while he was here.

"No, keep it on," he told me as he put the supplies down next to me at the foot of the bed. "It'll distract you while I'm getting this cleaned and dressed. And it's been forever since I've watched *Alias*. It'll be fun to listen to."

I obeyed, turning the show back on. Lennon went to the sink and got a basin of soapy water. Then he came back and dunked a washcloth in the water and wrung it out.

"I'm sorry if this hurts," he said as he started to wash my leg, wounds and all.

"It's okay. God damn it," I hissed as he hit a raw patch of skin that may or may not have had a cut on it. I couldn't even tell where I had cuts on my leg anymore.

"Sorry," he murmured. "Focus on Sydney and Vaughn, not on me. Trust me. It helps."

I chuckled weakly. "Sydney and Vaughn make everything better."

"What episode are you watching?" he asked as he continued working.

"'APO: Part One.'"

"Oh, you mean where the show started to get stupid?"

"Hey! I loved season four. What I was mad about was the two-year time gap that she had no memory of in season three."

"Right. I forgot you're a girl," he teased. "You cared more about the love story than the action, didn't you?"

"Guilty. Even though I don't feel much like a person, let alone a girl, these days. I can't remember the last time I felt anything at all other than pain. Fuck an ugly duckling!" I groaned as he cleaned one of the open wounds.

"I'm sorry. I know it hurts," he said softly, halting all movement for a moment before moving on to a different part of my leg.

Why had I just admitted that I felt less than human to him? Saying things like that in a hospital could land me in the psych ward.

But then I risked a look at Lennon's face. It almost looked like he was on the verge of tears.

Except that he couldn't have been. He was a guy doing a job. That was all. He was just being nice, and he was talking to me about my favorite show because he knew he could use it to distract me.

Whatever this thing was that I felt with him, it wasn't real. After I left this place, I'd never see him again and he'd forget all about me by the next day. And I needed to remember that.

five

hope

My daytime nurse had just left after giving me my morning meds when I heard the familiar ping on my cellphone that told me I had a Facebook message. Taking a deep breath and bracing myself, I sat the bed up…with all the groaning and whimpering and hissing that came with any form of movement these days. I wasn't allowed to have any more dilaudid for another hour – because, thankfully, the new internist that was assigned to my case had agreed that I could stay on that for the time being – and the dose Lennon had given me at about two this morning was wearing off fast.

I managed to grab my phone off my tray table, but I had to just lie there, half-up and half-down and panting for breath, for a couple of minutes before I could even muster the strength to lift my phone up and look at the message.

PEYTON

How are you feeling this morning?

ME

Um...the dilaudid from last night is wearing off and now I'm back to just wanting to beg someone to saw my damn leg off and be done with it.

PEYTON

🔔 I'm so sorry. Is there anything I can do from the other side of the country?

ME

Can you maybe check what takeovers I have this week and message the organizers to let them know I'm in the hospital and can't participate?

I saw the three dots bouncing, indicating she was responding, but before the message came through, there was a knock on the door and my nurse today, Kylie – who already seemed *way* nicer than Linda – walked in, accompanied by someone in tech scrubs and...

Oh, shit. I recognized the other nurse. It was Gina, one of the nurses from the wound care center.

My stomach twisted into a knot and bile started creeping its way up my throat as tears stung my eyes and my fingers curled around the side railing of my bed. I knew she was here to do a job, and I knew it was necessary for me to get better, but every single cell in my body was on high alert. If I could have physically managed it, I would have run out of this room screaming rather than endure what was about to happen.

"Hi, Hope. I'm Gina, one of the wound care nurses. I met you in the wound care clinic a while back. Can I take a look at your leg?"

I just nodded, afraid that if I tried to speak, I'd end up blowing chunks on all three of them.

"Is it the same wounds giving you problems as before?" she asked as she pulled off the dressing Lennon had applied last night.

"Yes," I choked out. "It's worse."

Gina went to the sink and grabbed a basin and some washcloths, filling it up with soapy water to wash my leg. Unlike Lennon, who had been so mindful of my pain, she didn't seem to give a shit. She roughly scrubbed every inch of my leg, and it felt like she was rubbing sandpaper over my wounds and then pouring vinegar over that. I was sobbing by the time she was done…and she hadn't even really started yet.

When I saw her grab the long one-ended cotton swab with a wooden stick on the other end, I swallowed hard to keep myself from throwing up.

"Please…please don't probe it," I whimpered. "I can't. It hurts too much."

She let out an exasperated sigh. This wasn't the first time I'd asked wound care not to stick things in my wounds because the pain was too unbearable. I knew logically that they needed to pack the wound – and that they had to measure how deep it was before they could do that – but I honestly just couldn't deal with that kind of pain right now.

"I have to pack these wounds, or they won't heal. That's why it got this bad."

Oh, really? That was why? Because wound care had been packing them before, and as far as I could tell, it had accomplished bupkes. If I'd started to go septic from this infection, I was pretty sure these wounds had been infected for a damn long time…and they'd never so much as given me a fucking Z-pack for it. They'd told me the pain couldn't possibly have been that bad and insisted that the smell and discharge were normal for lymphedema patients.

So, yeah...I was pretty sure that was why it had gotten worse, not because the wounds hadn't been packed. Granted, not having them packed probably hadn't *helped* the situation, but it definitely hadn't been the only contributing factor.

But I knew telling her that wouldn't accomplish anything. And the fact was, she was right. They did need to deal with this now, no matter how much it would hurt me.

"Can I at least have some lidocaine gel?" I sniffled as I accepted the inevitable.

"It won't work in time. Just grin and bear it. It'll be over before you know it."

And with that, she jabbed the wooden end of the cotton swab deep into one of my wounds, and I let out a cry of pure anguish as my entire body jerked off the bed.

"FUUUUUUUUUCK!!!" I screamed at the top of my lungs as my leg involuntarily started to pull away.

"Keep it down. It doesn't hurt that much," Gina huffed as she pulled the stick out of the first wound and moved to the second one.

I hated when people said shit like that to me. Were they in my body? Did they know how it felt to have three big, deep holes in their leg, which I was half-convinced had actually started to die and rot away?

No. No, they didn't. So they didn't get to tell me how much it fucking hurt.

"SON OF A BITCH!" I wailed as the tears started to stream down my face.

I had absolutely nothing to compare this pain to, but all I knew was that every single molecule in my body was screaming for relief that wasn't coming. My whole body was tensed up while my fight-or-flight reflexes begged me to run far, far away and spare myself from any further trauma. But all I could do was lie here and take it...in the name of "healing."

"MOTHERFUCKER! STOP! PLEASE! I CAN'T!" I yelled, panting for breath in between sobs as she stuck the swab in the worst wound.

"You need to be quiet. You'll disturb the other patients," Gina scolded me like she was talking to a five-year-old. "And keep still. It's not that bad."

Keep still? Was she fucking joking? I would have liked to see her deal with this kind of pain and not do what I was currently doing. It wasn't humanly possible.

Still, I lay back and gripped the siderails on my bed like a vise, sobbing uncontrollably and unable to catch my breath as she plunged the swab inside the wound again.

"Kylie, can you grab me some Silvercel, scissors, abdominal pads, Kerlix, and Tubigrip?"

"Absolutely," Kylie said, then disappeared out of the room.

She was back within three minutes, and then the pain and screaming and crying started all over again as Gina cut frighteningly long strips of the silver alginate and then shoved them as deep into my leg as they would go. Then she layered thick abdominal pads over the wounds and wrapped two full gauze rolls over almost my entire lower leg before covering it all up with a Tubigrip stocking.

"Okay, I'll be back tomorrow," she announced, and I wasn't entirely sure if she was talking to me or Kylie. "Keep that on as long as you can, and if you need to change the outer dressing, make sure you leave that Silvercel packed in the wounds."

"Got it," Kylie said.

"Is…is there anything you can do for the pain next time?" I asked timidly, knowing she'd probably dismiss it just like she'd done today.

I saw Gina roll her eyes, and I wanted to slap them right out of her head. Why the fuck had she chosen wound care as a specialty if she didn't want to deal with patients who were in pain?

"Not really," she said, her voice oozing with fake sympathy.

"The lidocaine gel won't have time to work, and I'd just have to stick the swab in your leg an extra time to apply it anyway. And we can't give you a local anesthetic because we can't stick a needle in your leg."

More tears started to sting my eyes, but I swallowed them down. I was *not* going to cry any more. Not in front of her.

"I'm on for the next few days," Kylie chimed in. "Can you call me about half an hour before you think you'll be coming? Then I can make sure she's had her dilaudid by the time you get here."

Gina nodded. "I'll make a note on the chart."

She walked out of the room, and I turned to Kylie.

"Am I allowed to have more pain meds yet?" I asked. "It still feels like someone jabbed a white-hot fire poker in my leg."

She checked her smart watch and nodded. "I'll put the call in to the pharmacy. By the time it gets here, you'll be able to have it. Did you get a chance to order breakfast yet?"

I shook my head. "You guys came in before I could."

"Okay, go ahead and order something, and make sure you call me for your insulin before you eat. Dilaudid can make you sick if you have it on an empty stomach."

Oh, I knew that all too well from yesterday. I'd been *so* nauseous by the time I'd gotten up to my room after having the dilaudid in the E.R. on an empty stomach.

After Kylie left, I found my room phone and called to order my breakfast. I really didn't have much of an appetite, but I knew I needed some protein after barely eating anything yesterday.

When I took a look at the menu, I found that I'd been put on not just the diabetic diet, but the *cardiac* diabetic diet…despite not having a history of heart problems *ever.* I didn't care so much about my limited food choices because I knew they were watching my blood sugar closely, but what I did care about was some assclown taking away my ability to have coffee. I was miserable and in the fucking hospital, and now I couldn't even have a damn cup of shitty coffee with my breakfast.

Another knock sounded on the door, and I looked over, hoping it was Kylie with my pain meds. But instead, an older man wearing a doctor's coat walked in, followed by two women in nurse scrubs.

"Hi, Miss Morrison. I'm Dr. Buchanan, the vascular specialist. They asked me to come do a consult for your leg."

"Hi," I mumbled.

"I took a look at the ultrasound they did in the E.R. yesterday, and I'm not seeing any blood clots or blood flow issues."

"I had a feeling," I sighed.

"I'm not seeing anything we can do for you. Really, the only reason you were admitted was for pain management."

Wait. What?!

That wasn't why I'd been admitted. Yes, pain management was part of it, but I was on IV antibiotics because I'd been flagging for sepsis from my infected wounds. *That* was why I was here.

"Since you're here, though, I am going to have lymphedema therapy and physical therapy come see you," he continued before I could say anything to correct him. "And I'm also going to put in a consult to general surgery."

Dr. Buttfuck gave me a pointed look, like he was expecting me to say or do something, but I had no idea what.

"Okay…" I said slowly.

"Do you know *why* I might be putting in a consult for general surgery?" His voice was so condescending and dripped with disgust and judgment.

That was when it hit me. What could I say? Being in so much pain that I could barely put a coherent thought together had made me a little slow on the uptake.

This fucking asshole hadn't even bothered to read my whole chart – not even enough to find out why I'd actually been admitted to the hospital – but he already thought he knew the answer to all my problems. And right now, when I was literally stuck here with nowhere to go, he was going to try to force it on me.

But if he thought I'd be grateful for his so-called help, or even just lie down and take it since I was stuck in this bed right now, he had another think coming. I'd just had deep wounds packed with zero painkillers or anesthetic and then found out I wasn't allowed to have fucking coffee while I was here. I was all out of fucks to give.

"I'm fat, not stupid," I bit out icily. "I *know* I need to lose weight. But if you want to help me with that, why don't you start with the extra *hundred pounds* in my leg instead of trying to permanently alter my digestive system?"

"Your leg doesn't weigh a hundred pounds," Dr. Bitchnipple practically growled at me. "And this lymphedema was brought on by your morbid obesity. If you ever want it to get better, you *need* weight loss surgery."

I pulled the blanket and sheet off of my legs. If he wanted to sit there and pass judgment, he was going to look at exactly where doctors telling me weight loss surgery would solve all my problems had gotten me. If he was going to be disgusted by me, then he was going to be disgusted by the truly hideous thing about me: my deformed leg that made me look like I belonged in a circus sideshow attraction. The product of years and years of seeing doctors just like him for my condition. *Not* the extra weight around my midsection.

"Yes, it does weigh a hundred pounds. And what I *need* is lymphedema therapy." My voice strained as I tried like hell to keep the tears that were stinging my eyes at bay. This fatphobic, misogynistic fuckwad did *not* get to see me cry. "I'm eating well, I'm managing my diabetes, and I've been trying like hell to lose weight, but I keep gaining it instead because my leg just keeps getting bigger. So *please* get me the help I need for my lymphedema and keep your opinions about my weight to yourself."

I swore I could *see* the steam coming out of Dr. Blowhard's ears as I spoke, but he didn't say anything to me. Instead, he turned to the nurses who had come in with him.

"Get her leg wrapped up tight in ACE wraps and bring in some more pillows to elevate it," he barked.

Oh, my fucking God. Where had this motherfucker gotten his medical degree from? Vascular doctors were supposed to be the most knowledgeable specialists when it came to lymphedema... and he'd just told them to do the *one thing* you were never supposed to do with this condition. ACE wraps had too much elasticity and didn't provide the kind of even compression a lymphedema patient needed. Using them would cut off the circulation to my leg and create divots and lobules that would be so much harder to deal with.

"No, it needs to be short stretch wraps," I said. "I'm not supposed to use ACE wraps on my leg."

Dr. Bukkake glared at me with narrowed eyes, like he didn't think I was even worthy to be breathing the same air as him.

"Listen to me, not her. *I'm* the doctor," he snapped at the nurses, then stormed out of the room.

As the nurses got to work doing the one thing that could possibly have made my condition worse, I looked around for my cellphone. I finally found it lying next to me on the bed and picked it up to find a ton of messages from Peyton.

PEYTON

> OMG HOPE!!! WHAT'S GOING ON???

> ARE YOU ALIVE???

> Are those assholes helping you? What can I do?

> Please tell me what's happening. I'm freaking out over here!

It was only then that I noticed the audio call within the Messenger app. An audio call that I hadn't knowingly made.

And judging by the time stamp on it...I'd been smack in the middle of getting my wounds packed when it happened.

Oh, God. Peyton had heard everything. And I'd had no idea.

I looked to see if she was online, and the green bubble next to her profile picture was faded, telling me that she'd been logged off for the past twenty minutes.

Damn it! I usually didn't message her when she wasn't online because I didn't want to take the chance that her husband would hear that prepaid phone go off or see the message. But after what she'd heard, I couldn't *not* say something. Especially since I had a feeling I was going to pass out as soon as the dilaudid took effect.

ME

> I'm alive. Wound care was here packing my wounds and I must have pocket dialed you. I'm so sorry you had to hear that! 🤦 🤦 🤦

> My nurse is coming in with dilaudid, so I'm probably about to pass out again, but I'll message you when I wake up.

Much to my surprise, my phone dinged with another message almost immediately.

PEYTON

> Thank fuck you're OK. Get some rest. Talk later. 🤍

I took a few deep breaths and swallowed hard, trying to keep myself from crying, but I wasn't entirely successful. Because, once again, I'd been judged and sentenced in the court of medical opinion. By people who were supposed to be helping me get better.

six

lennon

Note: The song "Unwell" by Matchbox Twenty plays a significant role in this chapter. If you don't know it, I highly recommend listening to it to get the full effect.

O n the side of the road near an exit on Interstate 405 stood a small white cross. A monument to someone who had lost their life on this highway, and a subtle reminder for everyone driving past it to be careful behind the wheel. Thousands of people passed by it on any given day, and of those thousands, maybe a tenth of them even noticed it and spared a fleeting thought for the people involved.

But for me? That cross represented agony. The day my life as I knew it had changed forever. The day the woman I loved had been ripped away from me, while nothing short of a miracle had kept her best friend, my sister, from dying right along with her. And twice a week, as I drove past it to visit Star in the rehab center she'd been living in since getting released from the hospital, it all came rushing back just like it was yesterday.

Today was one of those days.

As I pulled into a parking spot at Northwest Rehabilitation, I took deep breaths to try to alleviate the tightening in my chest. The tears building up just beneath the surface. The flood of heartache and sorrow that permeated every cell of my being whenever I thought about that night.

I took a deep breath and got out of the car, grabbing my guitar out of the backseat and steeling myself as I walked through the front door of the inpatient rehab facility. Taking the elevator up to the fourth floor, I made my way to Star's room.

A huge smile spread across my face as I saw her taking slow, labored steps down the hallway, hunched over a walker. Her physical therapist, Sean, was right beside her, pushing an empty wheelchair.

Even these tentative steps were more than we'd dared to hope for. After the car accident, Star had been told by several spinal surgeons that she might never walk again. And then, two months later, she'd started to get feeling in her legs again. She'd been determined every day since to regain as much mobility as possible, though her doctors and therapists had warned her she would probably never be one hundred percent ambulatory again.

My baby sister was the strongest person I knew, and even though coming here to see her brought back painful memories that I was still working through with my therapist, I was determined to support her every step of the way.

"Hey, you," I murmured as I approached them.

Star looked up and attempted a smile, though pain was evident in her creased brow and set jaw. "Hey. Perfect timing. I'm just about done."

And then her knees buckled, and Sean's hand zapped out and grabbed the gait belt around her chest to catch her.

"You're okay. I've got you," he assured her. "I think that's enough walking for today."

I quickly grabbed the wheelchair he'd been pushing and positioned it behind Star, and he guided her to sit down.

"Let's get you back to your room, Star," he said softly. "You did great today."

"Thanks," she panted as she tried to catch her breath.

"Do you want to try sitting in the recliner for a little while, or are you ready to get back in bed?"

"I…I don't think my back can take the recliner right now," she said apologetically.

"That's okay. This is a marathon, not a sprint. Let's get you into bed, and then you can just enjoy your time with your brother."

As Sean started to wheel her back into her room, she glanced down at the guitar case in my hand, and this time her smile was one hundred percent genuine.

She'd always hated that I had given up playing music when I'd started nursing school. But the sad reality was, there were only so many hours in the day. As much as I loved music and missed being the front man for Valiant Echo, a band I'd started with a few of my best friends in high school, I'd been planning a wedding and had chosen to guarantee myself financial stability rather than pursue my passion.

And now here I was with more than one broken dream, just going through the motions of life. Barely even able to remember what being happy felt like anymore.

My therapist, Jacob, had been the one to suggest picking the guitar back up, even if it was just for fun. So I figured maybe I could bring a little joy back into Star's life too.

"You're playing again?" she asked as Sean helped her transfer from her chair to the bed.

"A little. Jacob suggested it might help me. I was kinda hoping you might want to sing a few songs with me. But it's okay if you're not up to it."

She grinned. "I'd love that. What'd you have in mind?"

While Sean walked out of the room and shut the door, I got my guitar out of its case and did a little quick tuning. Then I played the first few *very* recognizable notes of one of her favorite songs to dance around in her bedroom to when we were in high school. A song I'd taught myself specifically for this occasion.

Star started giggling. "Oh, my God. You're ridiculous."

I chuckled. "Come on, you'd better sing with me. I'm not about to sing Taylor Swift all by myself."

She rolled her eyes, but chuckled. And this time when I started to play "We Are Never Ever Getting Back Together," she started to sing immediately, even accenting it with the trademark sarcastic remarks and spoken bridge. I didn't even have to sing – which I was grateful for, because I was most decidedly *not* a Taylor Swift fan. I went right into "You Belong With Me," another of her favorites, and again, singing was completely unnecessary because she nailed it from the first line. But when I started to play a third song, she stopped me.

"As much as I love Taylor, I know you hate her," she said, raising an eyebrow at me.

"I don't *hate* her. Especially not if playing her songs is making you happy," I countered.

"Then why are you so closed off?"

"I'm not closed off. Just tired. I like working overnights, but it throws my sleep schedule all out of whack."

"That's not what I'm talking about, Lennon," she said softly. "I don't think your therapist suggested getting back into music so you could learn a bunch of Taylor Swift songs to sing with me. He wanted you to have an outlet. A way to let your emotions out. And that's why I've always loved listening to you play music. When you sing, like really sing, I can *feel* it. You put your whole heart and soul into it. So do that now. Let your pain out."

I sighed. The sad truth was, I wasn't so sure I had that in me anymore. I wasn't sure I was even capable of the kind of emotions I used to tap into when I sang. It felt like that part of me had died with Candace.

Until last night.

Before I even consciously thought about it, my fingers were strumming the melody of Matchbox Twenty's "Unwell." This song had meant so much to me and Candace, helping us remember to hold onto each other when it felt like everything was falling apart.

But as I sang, I realized that this song had a completely different meaning to me now. It felt like every single word of it was about Hope. How desperate and miserable and alone she felt, and how she'd been ignored and overlooked by the people who were supposed to be helping her get better. And how what she needed right now was someone to stick by her and help her through this dark time so she could get back to being her old self, or at least get on a path to embracing her new normal.

I knew she had April, and I was so grateful she did because April was one in a million. Still, I couldn't shake the feeling that *I* was supposed to be there for her too.

"Lennon. Oh, my God. I wish I could get up and hug you right now. I haven't been able to listen to that song since…" Star trailed off.

I let out a weak chuckle as I set my guitar down, wiped away the lone tear that had started to trail down my cheek, and stood up to give her a hug.

"Me either. But…I wasn't singing about her. Not really."

"Coulda fooled me," she said, staring me right in the eyes as I backed away and sat back down.

I sighed. If there was one person in the world I trusted enough to talk to about Hope, it was my sister. And, frankly, I needed someone to help me screw my head on straight. I couldn't walk into work tonight still feeling like this. I couldn't let myself get in any deeper than I already was. Hope was my patient, and if I was going to continue to work on her case – and I felt like I needed to be, because she needed *someone* in her corner who would treat her with the respect and dignity she deserved – I had to keep whatever this feeling was in check.

The hard part was figuring out how to explain it to Star without violating HIPPA guidelines, and without feeling like I was violating Hope's confidence. As long as I didn't mention names, I could tell her about Hope's condition, but her condition wasn't really what was important. What was important was how much my heart hurt for this woman I barely knew.

"I wasn't," I insisted. "It…it was about someone I met last night. At work. A patient."

Star's eyes got as big as saucers. "You got that emotional over *a patient*?"

I took a deep breath. "Yeah. I did. I can't stop thinking about her. She's been through so much and she was in *so* much pain. Like, worse pain than I can ever imagine being in. But I could tell her doctor and the daytime nurse didn't give a rat's ass about it because all she was given was basically one step above over-the-counter painkillers. And the worst part is, it all could have been avoided if her doctors and therapists had just *listened* to her years ago when her symptoms first started showing and gotten her the help she needed then. She was in tears, but she was still trying to smile and crack jokes. It broke my heart. I know it doesn't make sense, but—"

"It makes all the sense in the world," she murmured. "You're human, Lennon. You're allowed to have feelings. You're allowed to have sympathy for your patients. That's what makes you such a good nurse."

"It's not just sympathy, though," I admitted. "It's more than that. It was like…like from the second I met her, something was drawing me in. There was this pull that I've *never* felt before. I can't explain it. And I don't know how to make it stop."

"Maybe you're not supposed to. I'm a firm believer that sometimes the right people find you when you least expect it. So maybe the universe put this woman into your life in a way you couldn't ignore because you needed to meet her. Or maybe *she* needed to meet *you*. Maybe you were put into her life to make this hard time a little easier for her."

"It doesn't feel like that. It feels like…I don't even know."

"Love?"

No, that couldn't be right. Could it?

I'd literally *just* met Hope. Even if I was ready to think about putting myself back out there again – which I most definitely wasn't – there was no way my feelings for a woman I'd just met could be that strong already.

Star chuckled. "What? I thought you believed in love at first sight."

"I used to," I sighed.

"You still can. It's not fair, what happened. It's not fair that an exhausted and overworked semitruck driver stole the woman you loved and future you'd been planning with her, or that it's only by a miracle that I'm starting to walk again. But the accident was just that: an accident. A godawful tragedy that changed our lives forever. And it's been almost a year, Lennon. If there's one thing I know about Candace, it's that she'd want you to find a way to move on and be happy again."

"It doesn't matter," I muttered. "She's my patient."

"And?" She shot me a knowing smile. "It doesn't matter how you met her. What matters is how you feel. And I'm pretty sure you wouldn't have been singing 'Unwell' about some random woman you just met. Not with how much that song meant to you and Candace. This girl means something to you, and it's okay to admit that. I know you can't tell me anything more than you already have because of patient confidentiality, but it sounds to me like maybe she needs the fresh start just as much as you."

"Maybe," I said, shaking my head. "If I see her again after she gets discharged, maybe I'll believe that."

"Just promise me something?" Her eyes bored into mine, pleading with me to take her words to heart.

"What?"

"If the chance comes, don't be scared to take it."

Blowing out a long breath, I picked my guitar back up. This conversation had taken a bizarre turn, and I wasn't entirely sure how to feel about it.

"I need to head home and try to catch a nap before I work overnight again. One more song before I go?"

Star laughed. "Fine, deflect if you want to. But you can't fight destiny."

seven

hope

I knew I was supposed to be resting. Really, I did. But since I'd literally just woken up from a four-hour nap and it was now five o'clock, I needed something to keep me awake for a little while so I would actually be able to fall asleep tonight.

So, shuffling my go-to playlist of dad rock, I decided to start self-editing the first twelve chapters of Kellan and Meadow's story. I wasn't in the headspace to write anything new – especially since I now had a caffeine headache on top of everything else – but at least I could pretend I was doing something constructive.

I was two chapters in and jamming out to "Rebel Beat" by the Goo Goo Dolls when Kylie practically stumbled into my room, taking a few deep breaths as she leaned one arm against the wall. I started to close my computer, but she shook her head.

"No, keep your music on. I'm just checking on you," she

said in a strained voice, letting out a long breath. "It's quiet in here."

Oh, my God. This poor woman. She had to be absolutely swamped if the only way she could get a few seconds of peace was by figuring out which patient's room was the calmest and going to check on them.

"Stay as long as you need to," I told her. "Is there a song I can play on Spotify to help you?"

She smiled. "This is actually perfect. I love the Goo Goo Dolls. So, what are you working on?"

"Um, I'm an independent author. I'm working on my next book."

"Oh, really? What do you write?"

"Contemporary romance," I mumbled self-consciously.

Usually, when I told someone I wrote romance, it was followed by a weird look or an, "Oh...*greaaaat*..." Like they thought romance wasn't real literature. Never mind that romance was the single best-selling genre on the market. Or that it was way harder than it looked to write believable chemistry and make sex scenes hot rather than cringey.

But if I was honest with myself, I knew it wasn't my chosen genre that people disapproved of. They just disapproved of me writing it. They didn't think a woman who looked like me could ever write believable love stories because they didn't think anyone in their right mind would want to be with me.

And it was partially true. Now that I looked like this, I was a pariah. But the worst part of this whole ordeal with my lymphedema – worse than the pain, the loss of mobility, the fatphobia, or the dirty looks – was that this hadn't always been my life. I hadn't always been stuck in a broken, defective body. In fact, up until very recently, my life had been blissfully normal.

I remembered what it was like to have both of my legs be the same size. What it was like to be able to walk normally. Wear my favorite pair of jeans or a pair of shoes that weren't pool shoes...because those were literally the only kind of shoes

I could find that would stretch over my ginormous, swollen foot.

I remembered when I could go outside the four walls of my apartment. Sit on the ground – or, hell, *fall* on the ground – without worrying about how the fuck I was supposed to get back up again. Go out to dinner or a movie or a concert. Have a social life.

And I remembered Chad, the man I'd been with until a year ago. The man I'd thought I was going to marry. The man who had told me I'd turned into a hideous, fat slob and he couldn't stand the sight of me anymore right before he'd slammed the door in my face.

That was when I'd realized that I could kiss any chance of ever finding someone to spend my life with goodbye. When I'd accepted that the only happy ending I had any hope of seeing was one I would write for my characters.

But Kylie didn't seem like she'd even thought for a second about someone like me having the audacity to write love stories. In fact, she grinned.

"That's amazing. I'm a huge romance reader. Do you have any books I can check out?"

That made me crack a smile. "Yeah, they're pretty much anywhere you can find eBooks. My pen name is Hope Claire."

Her eyes almost bugged out of her head as she let out something between a gasp and a squeal. "Oh, my God! I just read *100 Reasons I Loved You* last week. It *broke* me, but it was *sooooo* good! I legit called my best friend as soon as I finished it and made her buy a copy."

I laughed. "Thank you. It's one of my favorites too. Caleb and Penny have my whole heart."

"No joke, it's one of the best books I've read this year. Um, anyway, is there anything I can do for you right now?"

"Not unless you want to sneak me some coffee and not tell anyone," I sighed.

"They're not letting you have coffee?"

I shook my head. "They've got me on the cardiac diabetic

diet."

"Do you have any history of heart problems?"

"Nope. I don't really care about the limited food choices because I get that they're keeping a close eye on my sugars, but I just want to be able to have a crappy cup of coffee with my cardboard-flavored food, you know?"

"Yeah, I'm getting you some coffee. There's no reason they should have done that. Cream and sweetener?"

Oh, thank God. My leg pain probably wasn't going anywhere anytime soon, but maybe at least this caffeine headache would let up now.

"Yes, please. Splenda. Or Stevia if they have that. Thank you *so* much."

"Of course. I'll be right back."

As soon as Kylie left, I grabbed my phone to text April.

ME

Soooo...how much will you hate me if I ask you to run by my place and grab something within the next couple of days?

APRIL

Woman, you're in the hospital. Your wish is my command. Whatcha need?

ME

It's not actually for me. It's for my nurse, Kylie. I was hoping you could grab one of my spare copies of 100 Reasons. We were talking just now, and she asked about my books.

When I told her my pen name, she said she read and loved that one, so I wanted to give her a signed copy to thank her for going above and beyond for me.

APRIL

Long blonde hair and brown eyes? About my height and build?

ME

Yep.

APRIL

Aww! She's one of my work besties! Want any other books for her?

ME

I'd love to give her 99 Problems too since that's the second part of the duet. But I can't remember if I have any copies of that one. I think I might be out.

And she's on for the next few days, so I don't need it right away.

APRIL

Since they had to put me on a different floor while you're there, my schedule got switched around. I'm on tonight, but off for the next three days after that, so I was planning to come hang with you tomorrow anyway. I'll bring them then.

I hated to admit how happy that made me. Being alone usually didn't bother me. I'd gotten used to it since I'd become disabled and homebound.

But being alone in the hospital? It was a whole different kettle of fish. Here, I didn't even have my sweet furry friends to keep me company, and no amount of trying to distract myself could make me forget that I was here because something was very, very wrong. Pretty much the only upside to this whole experience was that I was finally getting decent pain relief and catching up on some much-needed sleep.

Well, the only upside other than Lennon. Which was pathetic all by itself. Because, really, what sane woman would have immediately started crushing on the first healthcare professional who'd shown her a modicum of kindness?

ME

You're the best! Thank you! 🫶

APRIL

You doing any better today?

ME

Yeah, other than the wound care nurse packing my wounds with zero pain relief. And then the vascular surgeon, Dr. Baboon's Ass – I mean Buchanan – trying to make me get a gastric bypass and then making the nurses wrap my leg in ACE wraps even after I told them not to this morning.

APRIL

woman spitting out drink laughing GIF

Mike Tyson laughing GIF

smiley face rolling on floor laughing GIF

I just sprayed Diet Coke out of my nose laughing.

I snorted as I typed my response.

ME

Wow, with friends like you, who needs enemies? 😛

APRIL

I'm laughing at the name, not at him being...well, a baboon's ass. Because seriously, that motherfucker needed to retire 15 years ago. He's convinced anyone who isn't supermodel-thin is overweight and that's the cause of all their problems.

ME

Best part? When the lymphedema therapist came in a couple hours later, she was like, "OMG, what did they DO?!?!"

I swear there was actual steam coming out of her ears when I told her they basically forced the ACE wraps on me after I told them not to do it. She said she was going to give him a piece of her mind.

APRIL

Sheila, right?

ME

Yep.

APRIL

If she said she was going to talk to him, she will. She doesn't fuck around.

ME

I could tell. She didn't pull punches with me either. But I liked her a lot, despite the pain she caused me. 🌀

She ended up wrapping my thigh and then putting two abdominal binders wrapped in opposite directions over that to keep the wraps on.

I quickly backed out of the text thread and pulled up my camera. Pushing my tray table to the side and tugging my blanket off, I snapped a picture of my leg, which was now completely wrapped in short stretch wraps from toe to hip with the binders over my thigh.

ME

picture of wrapped leg

I'm a mummy now. A very sore mummy who's very glad they're letting me stay on dilaudid for the time being, because having these wraps squeezing my wounds hurts like a mother.

APRIL

I'm sorry you're still hurting so much.

ME

I knew the pain wouldn't magically go away in a day. I'm just glad the new doctor saw reason and let me stay on the good drugs.

APRIL

No joke! IDK who thought one Norco would be enough for that kind of pain.

The abdominal binders are genius, though! I wish I'd thought of that when we tried the zillion things that didn't work to keep wraps on you six months ago. It's not the traditional way to do lymphedema wraps, but it makes so much sense for someone with a big lobule like the one on your thigh.

ME

Right? I'm gonna have to invest in some of those when I get discharged.

APRIL

Look, I've got to jump in the shower if I'm going to make it to work on time tonight. I'll see you tomorrow, okay? Text if you think of anything else you want me to grab for you.

ME

> Okay. Thanks again. See you tomorrow. 🐕

APRIL

> Get some rest and feel better. 😴

A knock sounded on my doorframe, and Kylie walked in carrying a Styrofoam cup with steam coming out of the lid, plus a handful of creamers and little yellow packets.

"I know we *have* Stevia, but I couldn't find any, so Splenda it is. Sorry," she said with a small smile as she set my cup of liquid gold in front of me. "And Dr. Fisher is going to be in soon to chat with you, so I sent her a message to talk to you about your diet. See if we can't get some of those restrictions lifted for you."

"Thank you so much," I murmured. "You don't know how much I appreciate it. I have the *worst* caffeine headache."

"Girl, I can't go even a day without coffee. Denying you the nectar of the gods on top of all the painful treatments they're doing on your leg is cruel and unusual punishment."

For the umpteenth time in the past twenty-four hours, this small kindness amidst all the judgment and pain made my eyes sting. I swallowed the lump in my throat and picked up my cup to blow into it, masking the long, slow breath I was releasing to keep myself from bursting into tears over a damn cup of coffee.

eight

lennon

As I approached Hope's room with her next round of Vancomycin in hand, I heard Daughtry's "Waiting for Superman" playing faintly. Not loud enough to disturb anyone, but just enough for anyone walking past the room to hear it for a few seconds. Her door was open, but I still rapped twice on the doorframe before walking in.

I couldn't help the warmth that spread through my chest when I saw her sitting up in her bed, typing away on her computer while she bobbed her head to the beat, softly singing along. This was a complete one-eighty from last night, and I was *so* glad for it because I wasn't sure if my heart could have taken seeing her so miserable again.

"Hey," I said, making her jump slightly as she looked up from whatever she was working on.

"Jesus," she gasped. "Lennon. You scared me. Hi."

"Sorry. In my defense, I *did* knock," I chuckled, then held up the plastic pouch that contained her medicine. "I've got your next round of antibiotics. Cool if I get it hooked up?"

She nodded and gave me a small smile that made my heart swell, and I went to unhook the empty bag from her last round of antibiotics and prep the new bag.

I still couldn't understand why I felt so drawn to Hope and why just a little smile or laugh from her felt like winning the lottery. But the more I mulled over my conversation with Star this morning, the more I realized maybe she and my therapist were right. Maybe it was time to think about doing what I knew in my heart Candace would want: moving on and finding happiness without her. I knew there would always be an ache in my heart from what I'd lost, but that didn't mean I couldn't find a way to carry it with me into my future without being crippled by it.

I wasn't going to be stupid enough to do anything about whatever the hell this was while Hope was my patient, but if our paths crossed again after she was discharged...well, who knew? It wasn't like we had to jump into a relationship right away. We could just enjoy getting to know each other. If that was something she wanted, obviously.

"So, what are you working on there?" I asked as I worked.

"Um, I'm an independent romance author. I'm working on my next book," she mumbled.

That made me smile. I didn't know why, but I had absolutely no trouble picturing Hope writing love stories. Maybe from when I was teasing her about the love story in *Alias* last night.

"That's so cool. My sister's a huge romance reader. Do you have any books I can tell her to check out?"

She raised an eyebrow at me. "Are you allowed to do that? Since I'm your patient?"

Damn it. She was right.

"I mean, I don't have to tell her you're my patient. I can just say I heard about your books from *a* patient."

That made her chuckle. "Well, in that case, my pen name is Hope Claire."

No fucking way. Star had been ranting and raving about Hope's books for the past couple of years. This was too bizarre to be a coincidence. Right?

"Oh, my God. No joke, I don't have to tell her about you because she's already read everything you've written. You're one of her favorite authors."

"Seriously?" she asked, those beautiful hazel eyes going wide.

"Yep," I chuckled. "She'd be so jealous if I could tell her I met you."

"Or she'd be disappointed when she found out how pathetic I really am." Sadness laced her words as she continued. "I think I started writing love stories because that was the only way I was ever going to get a happily ever after. By living vicariously through my characters."

So much for my heart not breaking tonight.

Hearing the regret and pain in her voice made my chest tighten with an emotion I couldn't put a name to. I hated that she thought so little of herself that she couldn't envision ever finding the kind of love she wrote about in her books. That she'd been conditioned to believe her worth was tied to her weight, what she looked like, and this godawful condition that she'd begged for help to manage, only for her pleas to fall on deaf ears.

I wished to God that I could tell her she *would* find that kind of love. That I could tell her how much I wanted to be the one to show her exactly how she deserved to be treated. That I could pull her into my arms and kiss her until she forgot why she'd ever thought she wouldn't find someone who loved her exactly as she was.

Whoa. Where the hell had *that* come from?!

Get a fucking grip, Lennon. She's your patient, *remember?*

Just as I was about to get the IV tube hooked up to Hope's

port, the song changed…and I stopped dead in my tracks, frozen in shock.

"Unwell."

Out of all the songs that could possibly have started to play right now, while Hope and I were talking about how she didn't think she would ever get a happy ending, it was this song. *This song.* What were the chances?

I'd never been one to believe in the paranormal, but I couldn't help the niggling thought that maybe it wasn't chance at all. That maybe *none* of this was chance. That it was Candace trying to reach me in the only way she could. Trying to tell me that it was okay to think like this. That I was allowed to move on, and that I was allowed to feel this way.

"Sorry, I shouldn't have said that," Hope said quietly, breaking me out of my trance. "You're here to work. You don't need to hear about my pathetic lack of a love life."

Right. Work. That was a thing I was supposed to be doing.

"Don't apologize," I said quickly as I grabbed an alcohol swab out of my pocket and wiped off her IV port before screwing the tube on. "I told you last night, I'm here if you need to talk."

She gave me a shy smile. "Thanks. But you can still feel free to tell me to shut up whenever you want. I'm a rambler."

"Little secret? So am I. When I'm not working, that is. Do you need anything else right now? How's your pain?"

"Honestly? Having these short stretch wraps around my wounds is *killing* me."

"I'm sorry I have to ask this, but on a scale of one to ten?"

"Six? Maybe a seven? The pressure on my wounds is awful, and then the gauze over all the little cuts and rashes makes it feel like someone gave me a nice paper cut and poured lemon juice on it."

I snorted at the reference to one of Star and I's favorite cult classic movies. "So you're just mostly dead, not all dead?"

Hope giggled. "Yep. I'd better not catch you going through my clothes looking for loose change. Anyway, I think it's too early for my next dose of dilaudid, right?"

Chuckling, I pulled the hospital-issued phone out of my pocket and checked her chart. "I can't give you dilaudid for another couple of hours, but they've still got Norco on your med list, and it looks like they upped the dose from what it was last night. I know it won't do much, but at least maybe that'll hold you over until you can have the good stuff."

She nodded. "It's worth a shot. Thanks. Do…do you think you could bring me a snack when you give that to me? Norco makes me sick to my stomach if I don't eat anything with it."

I could literally *see* her shrinking into herself as she said that, like she was terrified to ask for food. Like she thought I'd be upset with her or tell her she didn't need to stuff her face with anything else.

The way people at this hospital treated plus-sized patients – hell, just the way the general population treated their fellow human beings who happened to be carrying a few extra pounds – pissed me off. So much. No one should ever have had to be afraid of being ridiculed just for asking for a snack.

But I knew the only way Hope would stop being scared to ask me for what she needed was if I showed her with actions and not just words that I'd never ridicule her or pass judgment. That she was one hundred percent safe with me, in every sense of the word.

"Absolutely," I said with a smile. "Anything in particular you'd like?"

"Um, maybe some peanut butter crackers? Or graham crackers. Or applesauce. I'm not picky."

"You've got it. I'll see what I can scrounge up for you."

"Thanks," she murmured.

As I walked out of the room and put the request for Norco in with the pharmacy before heading to see what kind of snacks I could find for Hope, I couldn't help letting my thoughts drift off to all the events of the day. Playing guitar and singing for the first time in almost a year. My conversation with Star, and then my conversation with Hope. Hearing "Unwell" come on Hope's playlist at exactly the right time.

It was pointless to deny it. I was drawn to Hope, like a moth to a flame.

But I had to figure out a way to keep these newfound feelings in check. If I didn't, if I started to lose my objectivity, then I'd be taken off her case. And I couldn't let that happen. She needed me too much.

The truth was, though, if I was completely honest with myself, I knew Star was right. I needed Hope too. Because for the first time since the accident, I wasn't numb anymore. I could *feel* again. And every single one of those feelings was about her.

nine

hope

"Hey, girl, hey," April singsonged as she walked into my room, holding two gift bags and a big backpack.

I grinned and paused the episode of *Alias* I was watching. "Hey. What's all this?"

"This…" She set one of the bags on my tray table. "…is for my work bestie."

Peeking inside the bag, I found both books in my *Second Chances in Hampton* duet: *100 Reasons I Loved You* and *I've Got 99 Problems…and You Ain't One*. I also discovered that April had raided my swag bin and put together a swag pack for Kylie.

"You found *99 Problems*!"

"Yep, I did. It might have been your personal copy because I didn't see any other copies of that one. But I looked it over

89

and it was in perfect condition, so I figured you could always get another author copy if it was. I also brought this for you to sign the books with." She pulled one of the sparkly green Sharpies I always used to sign books out of her pocket, then put the other bag on the bed next to me. "And *this* is for my real bestie. Open!"

"Aww," I chuckled, holding the arm that wasn't currently hooked up to an IV tube out for a hug, which she happily gave me. "Thank you. But let me sign the books really quick first. I just ordered my lunch, so I'm gonna need to call Kylie for my insulin in a little bit."

"Okay. Here, let me move this out of the way." April unplugged my laptop and took it over to the windowsill, setting it and the backpack down.

Finding my bed control, I sat up, and April helped me get my tray table into a comfortable position. Then I signed the books, writing a different personal message in each one to thank Kylie for everything she did not just for me, but for all of her patients.

After putting the books back in the gift bag, I grabbed the bag April had set next to me. Inside, I found two little plush cats – one black and one white – along with a couple of adult coloring books, a box of forty-eight colored pencils, a book of *New York Times* crosswords and a pack of mechanical pencils, a couple of boxes of Ritz sandwich crackers, and a bag of sugar-free Dove milk chocolates.

"Since they lifted your dietary restrictions, I figured you deserved some snacks to keep in your room and a treat that wouldn't spike your blood sugar. And I know you miss Syd and Vaughn like crazy, but I thought these little guys could keep you company until you get back home and can get real kitty snuggles," April said, wrapping an arm around me.

I sniffled softly as a few tears leaked out of my eyes at the reminder of my fur babies. "Are they okay?"

"They miss their mama, but I've been giving them *all* the snuggles when I'm home," she murmured, rubbing my shoulder.

"And I brought a couple of your t-shirts from your laundry bin to my apartment for them so they can still smell you."

"You actually found shirts that weren't covered in that disgusting crap that was coming out of my leg?" I said, letting out a watery chuckle.

She snorted quietly. "I might have had to dig a little bit. But I also did a couple of loads of laundry for you, so you've got clean clothes whenever you're ready for them. That's what's in the backpack."

That made a few more tears trickle down my cheeks, and I took a slow, calming breath so they wouldn't turn into a full-on cryfest. I tried to wipe the moisture from my cheeks without her seeing, but I should have known better. She was way too observant not to notice. Immediately, I was enveloped in an embrace.

"You're gonna be okay, sweetie," she murmured. "I know it sucks being here, but you're going to get the help you need, and the social workers here will be able to help you with resources for when you go back home too. And you're not doing this alone. I'm here, every step of the way."

"Why?" I choked out, my voice breaking from the tears that wouldn't stop flowing. "I don't deserve it."

April pulled back just enough to pin me with a stern look. "I *know* I didn't just hear one of the sweetest, funniest, most creative, and most genuinely kind people I know tell me she doesn't deserve a little extra help while she's dealing with a serious medical issue."

"I don't," I sobbed. "I'm a horrible friend. You're doing all of this stuff for me, and I can't do *anything* for you. I can't even leave my fucking apartment to go out for coffee or have a movie night with you because I can't drive or even get down the damn stairs by myself. What kind of friend makes the other person do all the work to maintain the relationship?"

"A friend who's still figuring out her new normal after losing most of her mobility because a bunch of asshat doctors wouldn't listen to her when she tried to tell them something was wrong," she murmured, wiping a few tears from my cheeks before handing me the box of tissues on my tray table. "That doesn't make you any less of an amazing human, and it definitely doesn't even factor into the equation when it comes to how I see you. You're my best friend in the whole world. My person. The girl who has single-handedly gotten me through *three* different breakups and wrote one of my exes into *99 Problems* just to kill him off."

I snorted out a laugh as I dabbed at my eyes, and then a knock sounded on the doorframe, announcing that my food was here. As soon as they dropped off my tray, I called for my insulin, and Kylie walked in less than five minutes later.

"April!" she exclaimed with a grin. "Hey, girl. We miss you around here."

"I miss you guys too," April chuckled. "Thanks for taking good care of my sister from another mister."

"I'm doing my best. Speaking of which…Hope, I've got your forty units of Novolog right here. I'm guessing you want to do the honors?"

"Yes, please."

She scanned my bracelet, then handed the syringe and an alcohol swab to me, and I pulled up my gown and jabbed myself before popping the safety slider up and handing it to her.

"Before you go, I actually have something for you," I said.

"For me?" she asked.

I nodded. "Mm-hmm."

April grabbed the gift bag that she'd moved to make room for my lunch tray and gave it to her. When she opened it, her eyes got as big as saucers as she pulled the two books out and read the messages.

"Oh, my God. I…I don't know what to say," she stammered. "Thank you so much."

"Check out the swag pack," April told her. "Hope's got some seriously awesome swag, and she designs it all herself. I may or may not have gone a little overboard when I raided the bin for you."

Kylie pulled the numerous stickers and bookmarks out of the little sheer drawstring bag, followed by a pen and lip balm that each had my logo on them.

"Wow, you designed all of this?" she asked as she looked at each piece individually.

"Yep. I do my own covers and formatting for my books too."

"That's amazing. You're so talented," she gushed.

"Thanks. It gives me something to do so I don't go stir-crazy being homebound."

And then she found my favorite little goody I that included with all my signed books.

"Ha! No way," she giggled as she pulled out the little rubber squishy penis with a smiley face on it. "I've been *dying* to get one of these!"

I laughed. "I have the sense of humor of a twelve-year-old boy. I couldn't stop giggling for a solid ten minutes when I got my first order of those. They have squishy boobs on that site too. I'm going to order some of those for when I release my first sapphic book later this year."

"That's great," she chuckled. "Seriously, thank you. This made my whole week. Um, I'm going to go put this stuff in my locker before someone asks me why I have a squishy peen out while I'm on the clock."

"Solid plan," I agreed.

"Do you need anything else before I go?" she asked me.

"Nope. I'm good. Thanks, though."

"Of course. Just call if you need me."

Kylie left, closing the door behind her, and then April turned to me.

"Feeling a little better now that you made Kylie's day?" she asked.

I nodded. "Yeah. I always love giving away copies of my books."

"I know. And that's one of the many, *many* things I love so much about you. Go ahead and eat your lunch, and then we'll find something to watch on your laptop and just relax for the rest of the day. Sound good?"

"Yeah, that sounds perfect," I sighed as I opened the packet of ranch and poured it over my chef's salad.

Ten

hope

While April and I were in the middle of binging the first season of *Criminal Minds*, I heard my phone ping with a message alert. Picking it up, I saw Peyton's profile picture, so I immediately opened it.

PEYTON

> I'm SO sorry I haven't checked in since I heard you sobbing during your wound care yesterday morning. Michael was off yesterday and wouldn't leave me alone for a single second. I literally ran into the bathroom to respond to your message so he didn't see it. How are you? Any better at all?

My heart broke as I read that message, the same way it always did when I was reminded of the very real danger Peyton lived with every day. It killed me knowing that someone I loved like family was suffering so much and there was absolutely nothing I could do about it. And it killed me even more that she felt the need to apologize to me for going radio silent while her psycho husband was home so he wouldn't know she had friends outside of *his* circle of acquaintances.

ME

> You know you NEVER have to apologize to me for not being able to talk.

PEYTON

> I know, but I still feel bad. You're stuck in the hospital. I wish I could have been here to chat with you and keep your mind off things. And you didn't answer my question. How are you???

ME

> I'm okay. Still in a lot of pain, but at least my new doctor saw the light and agreed to let me stay on dilaudid.

> Other than that, April's off today, so she's hanging with me. And I may or may not be crushing on my sexy night nurse.

PEYTON

> 👀👀👀

> Sexy night nurse??? Tell me more!

> Are they giving you sponge baths?

I snorted as I typed my reply.

ME

> Get your mind out of the gutter, woman! No, he's not.

> He's just been super sweet and has spent time talking to me. He talked me down from a ledge my first night here.

April tore her eyes away from Dr. Reid and Agent Morgan to look at me.

"Peyton?" she guessed.

"Yep," I chuckled. "I told her I may or may not be crushing on a certain night nurse, and she just asked if he's giving me sponge baths."

April started cackling. "Oh, my God. Well, tell her you hate to break it to her, but the techs usually do that. And by the way, you have a crush on Lennon and didn't tell me? I thought we were friends!"

I rolled my eyes. "Um, I already told you I thought he was hot on my first night here. Remember?"

"Thinking he's hot and having a crush are two *very* different things, missy," she teased.

My phone pinged with a response from Peyton.

"Ha! Saved by the bell," I shot back as I read the message.

PEYTON

> Aww! I'm glad you have at least one good nurse. 🐾

ME

> My day nurse for the past couple of days has been pretty awesome too.

She smuggled me coffee yesterday and then got the doctor to lift my dietary restrictions since my blood sugar's been in normal range since I've been here.

I ended up telling her about my books and it turns out she read and loved the Hampton duet, so I got April to bring me copies to sign for her today. Getting to see her face when she opened the gift bag gave me ALL the warm fuzzies.

PEYTON

I'm so glad! Good nurses can be hard to come by. And I also feel horrible that I didn't know all this already.

ME

Don't feel bad! Not even for a second! You know I would NEVER want you to put your safety in jeopardy, and especially not for me.

I saw the three dots bouncing for a moment, and then they stopped and another message came through…in a new secret encrypted conversation.

PEYTON

About that. I need to tell you something, but you can't tell ANYONE. Not even April.

My heart leapt into my throat. In all the time I'd known Peyton and all the things she'd told me about her situation, she'd never once used the secret conversation feature to encrypt our chats. Since this profile was kept secret from her husband and she only accessed it on her burner phone that he didn't know about, she'd always said she didn't feel the need. So whatever she needed to tell me, if she thought she needed to add that extra layer of protection to our conversation, I knew it wasn't good.

ME

> The only thing I've ever told her about you is that you're one of my best friends and my Wonder Alpha.

> Are you okay? What's going on?

PEYTON

> I'm pregnant. I just found out today for sure. Had to wait until M went to work so I could get the test and take it without him finding out.

Oh, my God.

Fuck. Shit. Motherfucker.

I knew her husband, Michael, had been obsessively tracking her menstrual cycles lately because he'd been trying to get her pregnant. And I also knew that while Peyton wanted to be a mother more than anything, she wasn't willing to bring a child into that environment. She was caught between a rock and a hard place with nowhere to turn.

ME

> OMG. I...fuck, I wish I knew what to say, Pey. I'm so sorry.

PEYTON

> I don't know what the fuck to do, Hope. I can't end it, I just can't, but I also can't bring a baby into this house.

> And even if I DID decide to end it, he'd kill me if he ever found out. I know he would. I'm sorry, I feel awful telling you all of this when you're in the hospital, but I don't have anyone else I can talk to about it.

ME

> I know you don't. Don't apologize. I just wish there was something I could do to help you.

Just as I hit the send button, I realized there actually might be something I could do. But it involved doing the *one* thing she'd asked me not to do: telling April. And her brother, Noah.

PEYTON

> I don't expect you to do anything. I just need to…fuck, I don't even know what I need.

ME

> Actually…I might have a way to help. But I'd have to talk to April and her brother. And it would involve figuring out a way to get you to Portland. Will you let me do that?

The dots appeared and disappeared over and over again, and my hands were shaking as I waited for her response. When it finally came through, I was relieved and terrified all at once.

PEYTON

> Yes, you can talk to them. But if this one thing doesn't pan out, I need you to drop it and let me figure it out on my own.

> I can't have him accidentally seeing a message from you about this. Promise me.

Yeah…that wouldn't happen. I'd never stop fighting to find a way to get her out of Michael's house. But I also wouldn't do anything to put her safety at risk.

ME

> I promise I won't message about it if you're not already in this chat with me. But you can't ask me to just forget that you're in trouble. I love you too much to do that.

PEYTON

> I know. And I love you too. I'm just not holding out much hope right now.

My eyes stung and I swallowed down a lump in my throat. I hated that she was in so much pain and that, right now, she didn't see a way out of it.

ME

> April's still here, so I'm going to talk to her right now. Is he working tonight? Can I message you back in a little while?

PEYTON

> Yeah, he's at work.

I set my phone down, hands still trembling, and took several slow, deep breaths in an attempt to calm my jittery nerves and racing heart.

"Hope?" April asked. "What is it? Do I need to call Kylie?"

"No, it's Peyton," I choked out, trying to take another

calming breath. "She needs help. Badly."

She paused *Criminal Minds* on my laptop and turned to me. "What kind of help?"

"Her husband's abusing her. Has been for years. Like, he's put her in the hospital multiple times and almost killed her once. But he's the nicest guy in the world to everyone else, and her parents think he hung the moon. She doesn't have anyone to turn to in New York because the only people he lets her see are *his* friends and family. And now she's pregnant and she wants to get out of there because she can't stand the thought of bringing a baby into that house, but she doesn't have anywhere to go. I hate to ask this, but I know Noah has that groundskeeper's cabin that's going unoccupied at the resort, and you said he was thinking about hiring some help. If I can figure out a way to get her here, do you think he might let her stay there and maybe pay her under the table for a little while so it can't be traced until she can get back on her feet?"

"If he doesn't, I'll beat some sense into him myself," she chuckled humorlessly as she pulled out her phone and hit a number on her speed dial before putting it on speakerphone.

"Hey, sis. What's up?" Noah answered on the third ring. "How's Hope?"

I let out a weak chuckle. "Hey, Noah. I'm okay. Still hurting, but I'm on the mend."

"Hey, you. Glad to hear it. Try not to scare my baby sis half to death the next time your leg decides it hates you, huh?" he teased.

"I mean, it pretty much always hates me, but noted. Look, as nice as it is to talk to you, that's not actually why we called. I have a friend who's in trouble, and I thought you might be able to help."

"Translation: you'd better help or I'll kick your ass," April added. "And you know I've been taking kickboxing classes."

He snorted. "Okay, so what exactly am I helping with?"

I proceeded to explain everything to him. How I'd met

Peyton, what her husband was like, and how badly she needed to get out of his house before he found out about the baby. And then I asked him about the groundskeeper's cabin on the resort his and April's parents had left them when they died.

"She can absolutely stay in the cabin for as long as she needs," Noah said immediately. "And I will happily pay her under the table to do some administrative work for me. God knows I need it. Do you need any help getting her here? Like a bus ticket so it can't be traced back to her?"

"I'm not actually sure," I admitted. "I figured I should probably see if you'd even be willing to let her stay there before I worked out the rest of the details."

"Actually…Noah, remember Mom's friend, Vera?" April chimed in.

"Fuck. Yeah. Her fiancé found her because he managed to get a cop friend to show him the security footage from the bus depot and he figured out which bus she got on. Thank God, her intake nurse at the E.R. managed to get a detective there without him knowing and he got locked up for attempted murder."

"And Michael actually *is* a cop, so he could access the security footage at the bus terminal in New York. So…what if we get Peyton two different bus tickets? One in the opposite direction, like to Maine or Vermont, and then one from there to Portland?"

"There's still the problem of security footage at the bus terminals," Noah said. "What if we have her take a bus to somewhere like five to eight hours away in the middle of nowhere? I'll fly there and rent a car to drive us back, but we'll take the very long, scenic route and zigzag a little bit. Maybe even stop a couple of times to switch rental cars. Then we can send him on a wild goose chase that'll be even harder to track. Charlotte can hold down the fort here at the resort for a week or so."

"Hope?" April asked. "Do you think Peyton would be comfortable with that? Being alone with a man she's never met?"

"I'll have to talk to her, but I think she would be. If I vouch for Noah, I think that'll be enough for her. Now we just need to figure out how and when we can get her out safely."

"Just let me know when I need to buy my plane ticket," he said.

"Thanks, Noah," I sighed in relief.

"Anytime. I'll talk to you girls later. And Hope, just focus on getting better. April and I have this covered. We'll get Peyton here safely. I promise."

A knock on my door distracted me from obsessively checking my phone to see if Peyton had messaged me again. I'd sent her a message with the plan April, Noah, and I had come up with, but aside from telling me she was fine with Noah picking her up and that Michael was attending a friend's bachelor party weekend in Atlantic City in ten days – which was a perfect opportunity for her to leave and get a head start before he realized she was gone – I hadn't heard anything else.

"Hey," Lennon said as he walked into the room. "I've got your nighttime meds, and some melatonin if you want it."

I nodded. "I need it tonight, or I'll never sleep."

He scanned all the little packets into the computer system, then handed me a paper cup with my pills in it, and I downed them all in one gulp. Then he gave me the syringe containing my insulin, which I also took. And then he took out a syringe of dilaudid.

"I saw your blood pressure was pretty high when Tamika took your vitals, so I figured you probably needed this too," he said with a sad smile. "Can you tell me where you're at on a scale of one to ten?"

Well…now that he'd mentioned it, yeah, my pain was back with a vengeance. But that wasn't the reason my blood pressure was so high. It was because I'd spent the past few hours trying to figure out a way to get one of my best friends away from her abusive husband.

I should have been relieved. Peyton would be safe soon, and she'd be able to get a fresh start in a place where she already had people who loved and supported her – and, most importantly, *believed* her.

But I wasn't. Because bringing her here meant that our friendship would no longer exist behind the safety of a screen. It meant that we would meet in person.

And what would happen then? What would she think when she saw how hideous and pathetic I really was?

The sad truth was, I knew the answer: I'd lose her. Just like I'd lost every other friend except April. Peyton would take one look at me, be disgusted, and want nothing to do with me anymore.

"Like a seven," I sighed. "But that's not the whole reason my blood pressure's high. It's been a weird day. I have a friend who's in trouble, and I've been trying to figure out how to help her."

Oh, my God. What was it with me and word vomiting around Lennon? This was turning into a thing, and I couldn't for the life of me figure out why.

Okay, so that wasn't entirely true. I knew why. It was because he made me feel safe, and he made me feel *seen*. Like I was an actual human being instead of just a bunch of whacked-out numbers on a chart. Just by listening, validating my emotions, and going above and beyond the call of duty, Lennon had become a lifeline for me.

And I couldn't let it continue. I couldn't let myself forget that the only reason I'd even met him was because he was literally getting paid to take care of me while I was recovering from being deathly ill, and that he was almost certainly completely disgusted by me and just being nice because he had to be.

"I'm sorry to hear that," he murmured as he wiped my IV

port off and administered the dilaudid. "When it rains, it pours, huh?"

I snorted weakly. "Yeah, pretty much."

"Just try to remember that *you're* important too. And right now, your body needs rest. Trust me, I get feeling like it's your job to take care of the people you love, because I do the same thing, but it's okay and even necessary to make yourself a priority sometimes. God, I sound like a horrible self-help book."

I couldn't help it; I chuckled. "No, you don't. I know what you mean. April and her brother agreed to help, so my work is done. But I can't just flip a switch in my brain and stop thinking about it, you know?"

"I understand that one hundred percent. Do you want to talk more about it?" he asked.

I almost said yes. *Almost.* But I knew I couldn't do that. Peyton's story wasn't mine to tell, and especially not to someone I'd just met three days ago.

"I can't. It's not my place to say anything," I sighed.

He smiled. "Okay. Well, just call if you need me. Do you want the lights off?"

"Yes, please. Thanks. For everything," I said with an answering smile.

"You are *more* than welcome."

Turning off the lights, Lennon left the room, and just as he was closing the door behind him, my phone pinged.

PEYTON

> I'm sorry I've been so quiet. I'm just wrapping my mind around all this. It's a lot, you know? And I'm so scared something's gonna go wrong.

ME

> I know. It's okay. Is there ANYTHING I can do to make this easier for you?

PEYTON

> Just focus on getting better and getting back home. Because I'm gonna hug you SO hard when I finally get to meet you in person, and I'd much prefer it if you're not in a hospital bed when that happens. 😘

That did it. A few tears started trailing down my cheeks.

Why the fuck could I cry at the drop of a hat lately? This was getting really damn old. I was usually able to control my emotions way better than this.

I couldn't help it, though. Because I knew – I just *knew* – that Peyton wasn't going to feel the same way about me once she saw me in the flesh.

But that was a trade-off I had to accept. No matter how much it killed me. I'd never be able to live with myself if something happened to her when I could have stopped it. Even if it meant the end of one of the truest friendships I'd ever known.

eleven

lennon
one week later

Rob Thomas's "Streetcorner Symphony" was coming from Hope's computer when I walked in with a bag of saline for her IV.

Over the past week and a half, I'd gotten used to hearing either Rob Thomas or the Goo Goo Dolls about seventy-five percent of the time when I walked into this room while Hope was awake. And every time a Rob Thomas – or Matchbox Twenty – song came from her computer, I got the same feeling deep down in my soul, every bit as strong as it was a week ago. The feeling that Candace was reaching out to me in the only way she could, telling me it was okay to feel this way about someone who wasn't her.

"Hey, Lennon," Hope said, flashing one of those smiles that

were starting to take my breath away…and that were gradually getting more and more genuine every time I saw her. "Let me guess. More fluids?"

I chuckled. "Yep."

Unfortunately, in the process of fighting her infections, her kidney function had started to decrease, probably just from the massive amounts of antibiotics we were pumping through her system and her recovering from sepsis. I knew the doctor and social worker who were handling her case were looking into options for her discharge – most likely to an inpatient rehab facility for a bit to get her lymphedema a little more under control before they transitioned her back home – but they weren't comfortable sending her anywhere until her kidneys were a little more improved. So, in an effort to jumpstart that process, they were pushing a *ton* of fluids through her IV.

"Before you get me hooked up, do you mind helping me get out of bed so I can use the bathroom?" she asked as she paused her music, unplugged her computer, and pushed her tray table out of the way. "I was just about to call."

"Absolutely," I said, putting the saline pouch on the counter and going to grab some gloves.

In the past couple of days, she'd gotten to the point where she could get out of bed with a walker. It was still a little bit of a production, and it was far from easy, but I was *so* proud of her for pushing through the pain and doing it anyway.

By the time I got back to the bed, Hope had almost turned herself sideways, but was having issues with her bad leg, which appeared to be freshly wrapped. How exactly Sheila expected her to be able to walk in this getup, let alone do things like use the bathroom, was beyond me, but according to Hope, Sheila was always dumbfounded as to how her thigh kept getting unwrapped over the course of the day.

"Damn it," she muttered as she tried to yank at the Velcro fastening the abdominal binder around her thigh, which was now closer to being around her knee.

"Don't worry about your wraps," I told her as I gently lifted her leg and helped her get it to the floor, then positioned the walker in front of her. "We'll get them fixed once you're back in bed."

Hope took a deep breath and nodded, then grunted as she braced herself on the walker and stood up. She took one step forward…and promptly lost her footing as the grippy sock Sheila had haphazardly shoved over the wraps twisted around her foot and the smooth part met the tile floor.

Operating on instinct, I zapped my arms out and wrapped them around her waist, holding her tight. And despite the reason she was in my arms, I couldn't help the feeling that slammed into me like a freight train. The feeling that she belonged right here for the rest of our lives.

The walker rolled forward a bit, and Hope started to flail in my arms as she slid a little more.

"Fuck!" she squealed as she tried her best to keep the walker in place.

"It's okay," I murmured, tightening my grip on her. "I've got you. You're okay."

"I…can't…shit!" she grunted as her bad leg slid again.

"I've got you, sweetheart," I promised. "I won't let you fall."

I didn't have the time or presence of mind to even begin to process the fact that I'd just called her "sweetheart." I'd never called a patient by anything other than their name before.

But, then again, I'd never caught feelings for a patient before either.

I was in way over my head. I was in so deep, I couldn't even tell where the surface was anymore.

"I've got you," I repeated, trying to shake that thought from my mind. I had *way* more pressing matters to attend to. "I'm not letting go. Can you try to stand up a little more?"

She struggled for a second, but managed to somewhat find her footing.

"Good job, sweetheart," I encouraged her. "You're doing

great. Now, can you take just take one step back for me? Then the bed's right there and you can sit down."

Hope slid her bad leg backward, and then I helped her lower herself to the bed. Even though she was sitting again, I could still feel her trembling in my arms, and her breathing was rapid and uneven and she had tears in her eyes. I wanted more than anything to sit here with her and hold her until she was feeling better, but if anyone walked in and saw her in my arms like this... well, at the very least, I'd be taken off her case immediately. So, using a kind of strength I never knew I possessed, I managed to let go and kneel in front of her, tilting her chin so she'd look at me.

"Hope, can you take a deep breath in for me?" I asked quietly.

She attempted to obey, but only managed a small gasp.

"That's good. One more. Breathe in with me, then hold it for a count of four."

I took a deep breath, and she tried her best to match her breath to mine.

"One, two, three, four. Now let it out slowly for a count of four." I let out a slow, controlled exhale.

We did ten more breaths before her breathing finally evened out. Then I straightened the sock on her foot so the grippy side was on the floor again.

"Do you want to try walking to the bathroom again, or do you want me to grab the commode out of the shower for you?" I asked.

"I...I think I just want to use the commode," she mumbled quietly.

"That's okay," I assured her as I stood and walked into the bathroom to grab the plastic chair with a bucket attached to it. "I wouldn't want to try walking again after I almost fell either."

"Why the fuck do they give us these damn rolling walkers? Lot of good it does if you actually need it to...I don't know, hold you upright," she grumbled.

I snorted. "You are *not* the first patient to point that out."

"Can you hold that side still for me so I can tighten this?" I asked once Hope was comfortably settled back in bed.

"Yep," she said, still a little out of breath, as she grasped one side of the abdominal binder that I'd moved back up to where it was supposed to be on her thigh.

Using all my upper body strength, I pulled the Velcro tight across her leg and fastened it.

"Fuuuuuuuck," she groaned.

For a split second, my mind went to a place it didn't need to go. A place that it was getting harder and harder not to let it wander to by the day.

I wondered what she'd sound like groaning that word in pleasure rather than pain. What kind of sounds she'd make while I devoured her like my last meal. How she'd sound screaming my name as I made her come undone.

"So, I saw on your chart that they're talking about discharging you to a rehab center tomorrow," I said, desperate to divert my brain to something else.

Something that didn't involve blurring the fuzzy line I was walking any more than it already was. For the second time today.

"That's what they're telling me."

Yep, that did the trick. Just thinking about the very real possibility that this could be my last night caring for her made my heart sink.

"They did an ultrasound of my kidneys today just to make sure there's nothing else going on other than just the infection and antibiotics messing with them," she sighed, bringing my attention back to the conversation. "But the doctor was gone by the time they were done, so I won't know the results until tomorrow. I kind of hate that. I don't do well having to wait for news. Makes my anxiety skyrocket."

"I know how that goes," I murmured sympathetically. "I'm the same way."

"Especially when they couldn't actually get a clear picture of them. Two things you absolutely *don't* want to hear while you're getting an ultrasound on your kidneys are, 'Have you ever had surgery on your kidneys before? Do you *have* both of them?' Literally, they said it exactly like that."

I let out a shocked chuckle, unable to believe the ultrasound tech had been so blunt and flippant about something that serious. Some of the people in this place really needed to go back to sensitivity training.

"Wow," I said with a snort. "I mean, what did they expect you to say? 'Oh, *that* explains the time I woke up in the bathtub in Tijuana.'"

Hope burst into a fit of giggles. Honest-to-God uncontrollable laughter. The sound was so infectious that I couldn't help but join in.

And this might have been my last chance to ever hear it.

"Oh, my God," she laughed. "I totally should have said that. I might have to steal that next time someone asks me a stupid question about whether I have all of my organs."

"Hopefully you'll never have a need for a one-liner like that again, but it's all yours if you ever need it," I teased.

"Thanks for that. Um, do you know when I can have my next dose of Percocet? I'm pretty sore after that almost-fall."

"Let me take a look." I took the hospital phone out of my pocket and pulled up her chart. "Looks like in about forty-five minutes. Can you hang in that long, or do you want me to see if we have any other options?"

She nodded. "I can wait. It's not unbearable. I'm somewhere between a five and a six. I just definitely can't sleep like this. Thanks."

"I'll be back with your nighttime meds in about an hour, so I'll bring it and a snack then. Sound good?"

"Yeah, that's perfect. Thanks," she said, flashing me another of those smiles.

As I walked out of Hope's room, I could feel my chest

tightening as my heart slowly started to break into a million pieces.

I knew exactly how fucked up that was. I knew should have been happy that she was getting better. That she didn't need to be here anymore. But all I could think about was how I might never see her again. Never get to talk to her again. Or see that beautiful smile.

Maybe this was all our relationship was ever supposed to be. Maybe I was supposed to comfort her and make this hospital stay a little more bearable for her, and maybe she was supposed to open my heart to the possibility of letting someone in again.

But it was never meant to be her. Because if she was the one I was supposed to let in, she wouldn't have been put into my life like this. As someone I'd eventually have to let go.

Twelve

lennon

Something was different.

I couldn't explain it, but there was an unfamiliar energy as I walked into the hospital tonight. Like something here had shifted suddenly.

If I was honest with myself, I knew what it was. I knew it, but I didn't want to admit it. Because then I would have had to process why my heart physically hurt from the mere thought of it.

But when I saw April back on my floor, there was no hiding from it anymore. Her being back on this rotation could only mean one thing: Hope had been discharged.

And I'd never get to see her again.

"Lennon!" April exclaimed with a smile. "Hey! I've missed working with you and Brady."

I forced a smile, but I knew she'd never buy it. "We've

missed you too."

She snorted. "Yeah, like a virus, I can tell."

"Sorry," I murmured, letting out a humorless chuckle. "It's not that I'm not happy you're back. I promise."

Her smile faded a little, morphing into something more… sad? Pensive? I couldn't tell. But it was still genuine.

"You're upset that Hope's gone," she guessed.

With a sigh, I nodded. It was pointless to deny it, especially to Hope's best friend.

"It sounds awful, I know," I told her. "I *am* glad she's gotten better enough to be discharged."

"But you like her," she finished for me.

I nodded again, and she just chuckled.

"It wasn't hard to see that when you came into her room while I was visiting. And I know exactly what you see in her. Hope's…God, she's the best person I know, but she doesn't see it. She's spent her whole life being talked down to by doctors, people who called themselves friends, and even her own family. So many people have told her that her worth was tied to her weight and the lymphedema, and she's started to believe it. I see it more and more every day. She needs someone like you. She deserves to get even a fraction of the happiness she wants for everyone else."

I'd picked up on that within less than an hour of meeting Hope. The self-deprecating jokes. Her fear of asking for pain meds or food to take her medicine with and of admitting how much she was hurting. It all pointed to her being conditioned to believe her needs and feelings didn't matter.

And then, of course, there was the one day that was permanently burned into my memory, no matter how hard I'd tried to forget it.

"The day after she was admitted, when I walked into her room with a dose of antibiotics, she was working on one of her books," I said quietly. "I asked about it, and she told me that she writes romance because she wants to live vicariously through her characters. Give them the happy endings she doesn't think she'll get. It broke my heart. I wished I could tell her she'd get her own happy ending one day. That I wanted to be the one to give it to her.

"I should have asked to be taken off her case that day. I knew I was getting too personally involved. But I just…I couldn't. Not when I knew most of the people here were treating her like shit. She needed someone here who treated her with respect and dignity."

She put a hand on my arm, squeezing lightly. "I'm glad you didn't ask to be taken off her case. Because you were right. She did need you. And *I* needed to know you were on her case so I didn't worry about whether my sister from another mister was getting the care she deserved here. But there's nothing wrong with admitting there was a spark or two, Lennon. She's not your patient anymore."

I sighed. April was right. Hope *wasn't* my patient anymore, so there was nothing wrong with admitting how I felt now.

But it wasn't like I could just go into Hope's file and find her address. Or even ask April where she was. That would have violated all kinds of patient confidentiality laws. I'd have lost my job, and probably my nursing license too. Unless we happened to bump into each other outside of the hospital – which was basically impossible since Hope was homebound – I would never see her again. Except, of course, if she got admitted again, which I definitely didn't want. Her health was more important than the gnawing ache in my chest at the thought of never seeing her again.

Apparently, April was putting all that together in her head too because an impish grin slowly started to spread across her face. "Listen, I can't tell you where Hope is because that would be unethical. But…I'm just saying that if you went to visit your sister and you *happened* to pass by room 342 while you were at that facility, you *might* see someone familiar."

I froze.

For a solid ten seconds, I lost my ability to move. To speak. To breathe. To *think*. At least not beyond the echoing of Star's words in my brain.

"Just promise me something? If the chance comes, don't be scared to take it."

"Fine, deflect if you want to. But you can't fight destiny."

April had just handed me *the chance* on a silver platter. I could see Hope again. Really get to know her outside the bounds of being part of her care team at Kingman Medical Center.

Now the only question was, did I have the courage to take it?

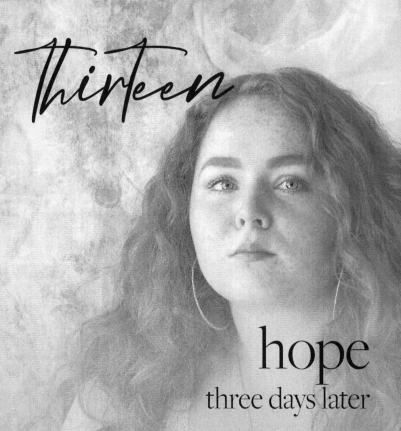

Thirteen

hope
three days later

Thank God today was Sunday.

I was exhausted after the past few days of being at leg boot camp. I'd had to agree to do two hours of physical therapy *and* two hours of occupational therapy a day on top of the lymphedema therapy for them to even accept me as a patient. Except on Sundays. I got to relax on Sundays.

I knew I needed the help because there was no way I could go back home to my second-floor walk-up apartment without building up at least enough strength to be able to get up the stairs on my own. And the therapy was broken into four one-hour sessions spread throughout the day, so I got breaks, but by the end of the day, I was always beat and sore all over. And then, to top it off, I had to get my leg wrapped at some point during the day too.

So, I was glad for the day to just relax, especially since Peyton was currently on a bus from New York City to Montpelier, Vermont. Noah had flown to Burlington and picked up a rental car at the airport yesterday, and he was going to meet her at the bus station when she got there at six tonight. The plan was for them to drive for at least a few hours before stopping at a hotel for the night just in case Michael managed to figure out where Peyton had taken a bus to.

I'd been jamming out to my favorite dad rock all day while chatting with her. And, well, to say she was nervous would have been the understatement of the century. She was so sure Michael would figure out where she'd gone, get a plane ticket, and be there waiting when she stepped off the bus. I'd tried my best to reassure her, but I knew there was nothing I could say that would take that fear away. She probably wouldn't really feel safe again for a long time, not even when she was finally living on the other side of the country.

My Facebook alert tone pinged, and when I checked the notification, I saw that someone had commented on a predictive text game I'd posted in my Facebook reader group. Since a couple of my books dealt with stalkers, I'd made a graphic with the line "I have a stalker because…" and then asked my readers to finish the sentence with the predictive text on their phones. And when I saw the latest response, I started laughing so hard I couldn't breathe.

> I have a stalker because he is a scam guy who has a grandma.

Taking a screenshot, I sent it to Peyton. If I couldn't calm her down during this bus ride, at least maybe I could distract her and make her laugh.

PEYTON
OMG he has a grandma! 🤣🤣🤣

woman spitting out drink laughing GIF

smiley face rolling on floor laughing GIF

Mike Tyson laughing GIF

Jimmy Fallon laughing GIF

Chris Evans laughing GIF

She must be SOOOOO proud.

Grandma, I'm a scam guy!

ME

You can't make this shit up.

PEYTON

You really can't. OMG I can't breathe.

My alert tone pinged again just as I'd somewhat caught my breath from laughing so much it hurt. And then the giggling started all over again as I read the next response, which I also screenshotted and sent to Peyton.

I have a stalker because I fell and broke my wrist and he braided my hair.

ME

> OMFG I didn't think anything could top that...but look at the one right below it. 💀 💀 💀

Instead of getting a text message back from Peyton, a voice message came through a few seconds later.

"He...braided...my...hair," came the voice I'd only heard a handful of times, barely intelligible through her laughter. "Oh...my...God!"

Still guffawing, I typed my response.

ME

> I almost want to post that screenshot and say anyone who can top it gets a prize. Because I don't think it can be done.

A knock sounded on my doorframe, and I looked over expecting to find a nurse or tech coming to tell me to quiet down. Except it wasn't a nurse. My cackling came to an abrupt halt as all coherent thought left my brain for a solid five to ten seconds.

"Le...Lennon," I finally stammered.

Lennon – looking so good it should have been illegal in a Matchbox Twenty t-shirt and ripped jeans rather than the scrubs I was used to seeing him in – took a tentative step into the room, setting the guitar case he was carrying down by the door.

Wait, he played guitar?

And did he know how much I loved Rob Thomas, or was it just a coincidence that he was wearing that shirt? Had he been paying that much attention to the music I'd played while I was under his care?

No, he couldn't have known. Right?

"Hey, Hope," he chuckled awkwardly. "I hope it's okay that I'm here."

I nodded quickly as I paused my music. "How..."

Dear God, why couldn't I form a coherent sentence?

"A little birdie told me," he said with a heart-melting smile as he rolled the oversized recliner they'd brought in for me closer to the bed. "My…um, my sister's actually a patient here, and when April got back to my floor a few days ago, she told me you were here too without actually saying it. So, I thought I'd come by and visit for a little while if you're up for it."

Why exactly a crushing wave of disappointment washed over me, I had no idea, but it did. So intensely that it was all I could do not to start crying.

Of course he hadn't come here for me. Why would he have? I was just a pit stop for him on the way to visit someone he actually cared about.

He had family. Friends. A life. And I had no one other than April and Peyton.

To him, I was just one person in a sea of patients. Someone he'd forget about by next week. But to me, he'd become a lifeline. No matter how much I'd tried to stop it, it had happened.

"Shit, that didn't come out right," he muttered, letting out another almost painfully awkward chuckle. "I wanted to see you again. You being in the same facility as Star just gave me an excuse. And April a way to tell me how to find you without breaking any laws."

Fuck. Me.

Had I really let my feelings show that much? I'd been a fucking wreck over the past couple of weeks, and now he pitied me, which was even worse than him just dropping by on the way to see his sister.

"You're that much of a glutton for punishment?" I said, deflecting with humor like always.

Instead of laughing like I'd expected him to, Lennon leaned forward and took my hand in his, giving it a small squeeze. "Sweetheart, getting to see you, getting to really talk to you… it's the farthest thing from punishment imaginable."

Damn it. There was that endearment again. The same one

he'd used during my last night in the hospital. The one that had made butterflies swarm in my stomach even though I'd been flailing around in his arms like a fish out of water while trying not to land flat on my ass.

And hearing it made a flicker of hope start to bloom deep in my chest. Hope that maybe he felt even a fraction of what I did every time I laid eyes on him.

"I didn't…I never expected to see you again," I murmured self-consciously.

Fuck, was that really the best thing I could come up with?

Not letting go of my hand, Lennon stood halfway and dragged the recliner even closer to the bed.

"Me either," he said softly as he rubbed circles over my hand with his thumb. "And that thought killed me. When I found out you'd been discharged from the hospital, my first reaction wasn't being glad that you'd healed enough to be transferred here. It was sadness that I'd never get to see you again. I knew how fucked up that was, but I couldn't shake it, no matter how much I tried. You've gotten under my skin, Hope. From the very first time I met you, you woke up something inside me that I thought was dead. It took me this long to come see you because I needed to wrap my head around how I felt. How I *feel*. And I needed to find the courage to tell you. To see if there's a snowflake's chance in hell that you feel the same way."

My chest felt tighter and tighter with every word he said, and by the time he was done, I was pretty sure I was going to explode from the pressure. Every breath was a struggle, and I knew – I just *knew* – that there had to be a punchline. A "gotcha" moment. Someone lurking around the corner who was about to pop out and tell me I'd been *Punk'd*. Because there was no other earthly reason why a man who was built like a Greek god and was as kind and caring as he was would have even wanted to be in the same room with someone who looked like me, let alone been telling me that he had feelings for me.

But I couldn't find the words to say any of that. Instead, only four words escaped my lips.

"Why, Lennon?" I asked on a trembling breath. "Why me?"

He took a long inhale, then raised our still-joined hands and brushed his lips over my knuckles. "Because you're one of the most incredible people I've ever met. You're beautiful, you're kind, you have an amazing sense of humor, and you're so fucking strong despite everything life's thrown at you. I'm in awe of you, Hope."

Now I *knew* I was being *Punk'd*. Maybe this was his form of payback for making him take care of me while I was an inch away from dying. But I swallowed past the burning in my throat and blinked back the tears that were stinging my eyes. I couldn't cry in front of him. Not now. I had more dignity than that.

"Stop, Lennon," I croaked, unable to look at him for fear that I'd break. "Stop with the flowery words and the lies and whatever fucking game you're playing right now. Just *stop*."

Lennon's hand left mine and moved to my chin, gently turning my head until I had no choice but to meet his chestnut eyes. And what I saw there floored me.

He looked heartbroken, and this time, I knew there was no mistaking it. A lone tear slid out of the corner of his eye and trailed down his cheek as he spoke.

"I'll never lie to you, Hope," he whispered. "I promise you that."

"Then *stop* telling me I'm beautiful," I choked out, sniffling quietly. "I'm not stupid, Lennon. I'm not just obese; I'm *morbidly* obese. I can barely walk. I can't shower by myself because I'll slip and fall and won't be able to get back up without calling the fire department to help me. And my goddamn leg is so big it has its own fucking zip code. I might be a lot of things, but beautiful is *not* one of them."

If I'd thought he looked upset before…well, now he looked completely crushed and devastated. I swore I could actually *see* the cracks forming in his heart as I gazed into his eyes, pleading with him not to tell me things that we both knew weren't true.

Lennon opened his mouth like he was going to say something, but then shut it again and stood up.

Now that he'd had his fun and inflicted maximum pain, he was going to—

My spiraling thoughts were cut off as he took my face between his hands and crashed his lips to mine in a searing kiss that made me forget my own name, let alone why I'd ever thought he would be so cruel.

fourteen

lennon

Note: The song "Waiting for Superman" by Daughtry plays a significant role in this chapter. If you don't know it, I highly recommend listening to it to get the full effect.

Hope let out a startled gasp and froze for a second as my mouth met hers. And then she tentatively started to move her lips against mine and I swore actual fireworks went off behind my eyes.

I hadn't been planning on this today. Hell, I hadn't even intended to wear my whole damn heart on the sleeve of this Matchbox Twenty shirt I'd donned to show her we had something in common. I'd just wanted to talk to her. Get to know her a little more. But when the only words she could manage to get out were questioning everything I was saying to her and telling me all the reasons she didn't believe me, all my plans of taking it slow had gone out the window. I knew I couldn't leave *any* doubt in her mind about the way I felt.

I gently traced the curve of Hope's soft, perfect lips with my tongue, asking for entrance, and she parted them on a sigh, allowing me to search out her tongue and curl mine around it. Drinking down her quiet moans like they were life-saving sustenance, I took my time exploring her mouth, slowly but purposefully stroking my tongue against hers.

All the blood in my body rushed south, making my cock strain against the confines of my jeans, but despite this unexpected turn of events, I knew this wasn't the time or the place to take this any further. So, when I finally needed oxygen more than I needed her lips to stay connected to mine, I pulled back, brushing my lips against hers once more before looking her in the eyes and swiping away the few tears that had started to trail down her cheeks.

"Look at me, Hope," I whispered, keeping my hand on her cheek so she couldn't turn away as I planted a featherlight kiss on her forehead. "I need you to hear me say this. Really *hear* it."

Those hazel eyes I loved so much raised to meet mine, a mixture of fear, uncertainty, and cautious optimism swimming in them.

"I don't *ever* want to hear you talking about yourself like that again," I told her. "Not for a second. You. Are. Beautiful. Inside *and* out. Your weight and your lymphedema don't have a damn thing to do with how fucking gorgeous you are. If you'll let me, I will spend every day of my life telling you that until you believe it. And then I'll keep telling you so you never forget. Do you hear me?"

Hope took a couple of shallow breaths before giving me a timid smile. "Yes. But I still don't understand."

I was about to tell her everything. To try my best to explain something I didn't even fully understand myself. But then her phone buzzed with a notification, and she let out a gasp as she checked it.

"Shit. Peyton," she muttered as she started tapping on the screen. "I'm so sorry, I have to respond to her. She needs me."

I lowered the side rail on her bed and started to sit down, and she scooted over a little to give me more room – something that just two short weeks ago, she wouldn't have been able to do. It was incredible how far she'd come, and she didn't even see it.

"You don't have to apologize, beautiful." I trailed a finger up and down her arm, unable to stop touching her now that I was finally allowed to. "Is she who you were texting when I walked in on you laughing your ass off?"

She let out a cute-as-fuck little snort as she put her phone down and turned back toward me. "Yeah. Um, she's the one I told you about like a week ago. The one who needed help. Her husband was abusing her and she needed to leave, but she didn't have anywhere to go. She's on a bus from New York City to Vermont right now, and April's brother, Noah, is meeting her there and they're going to drive here in a rental car. Noah's got somewhere she can stay for a while until she gets back on her feet. But she's *so* scared that her husband will figure out where she's headed and get there first, so I've been texting with her all day to distract her."

Holy shit. She'd orchestrated all of this from her hospital bed? Yes, April and Noah had played a role too, but coming up with an escape plan for a domestic violence survivor would have been a huge feat even for someone in perfect health. Yet Hope had figured out a way to help her friend while she was bedbound in the hospital.

"Why are you looking at me like that? Do I have something in my teeth?" she chuckled uncomfortably.

I smiled and leaned forward to kiss her forehead. "Nope. You just added to my ever-growing list of the things I love about you. I can't believe you did all that while you were in the hospital."

Hope's cheeks darkened as her gaze darted downward. Clearly, she wasn't used to getting compliments. Or at least she had a hard time accepting them. But I'd work on that. Help her to see what I saw every time I looked at her.

"Noah did most of it," she mumbled. "He's the one who's letting her stay in an empty cabin on the resort he owns, and he's the one who volunteered to fly to Vermont with only ten days' notice to help a woman he'd never even spoken to. All I did was ask him if she could stay there."

"That's still a hell of a lot more than most people would have done. And it sounds like more than anyone she knew in New York did for her. Don't sell yourself short, sweetheart. You're her hero. Well, heroine. I'm guessing that's an important distinction for a romance author."

There was that snort again. It was now in my list of my top three favorite sounds ever. Number one was her moans when I'd kissed her. Which I desperately wanted to do again.

"That it is," she chuckled. "The wild thing is I've never even laid eyes on Peyton before. I met her in a romance group on Facebook and we just clicked. Now she's like a sister to me. But I'm so scared to meet her in person when she gets here next week."

I knew she was probably expecting me to ask her why. But I couldn't do that because I knew exactly what I'd hear if I did, and I wasn't about to give her another opportunity to be unkind to herself. Not when I could intercept and redirect.

"She's going to love you," I assured her. "I'm sure she already does."

She blew out a long sigh. "I hope so. Anyway, tell me something about you. I feel like you know pretty much everything important about me, and I don't know anything about you. God, I don't even know your last name."

"McCartney. No, I'm not kidding."

"Wait, seriously? Your name is Lennon McCartney?"

"Lennon *Harrison* McCartney," I chuckled. "Triple whammy."

She giggled for a second, then stopped short. "Sorry. I shouldn't laugh. But didn't you say your sister's name is Star?"

I nodded. "Yep. Star Lucille. But at least they were kind enough to only spell it with one R. And you can laugh. We poke fun at our own names enough. She *hates* that she's named after a song about getting high off your ass. I swear our parents were just trying to be funny when they picked our names."

"*Please* don't tell me you have a brother named Ringo," she snickered.

"Nope," I laughed. "It's just the two of us. I don't even want to know what they would have done if we'd had any other siblings."

"With a name like that, I shouldn't be surprised music runs in your blood." She cocked her head in the direction of my guitar.

"Yeah, I was the front man for a band called Valiant Echo in high school. Me and my three best friends. But when I started nursing school, I kinda stopped playing for a while. I was just too busy. I only recently picked it back up. Really, I've just been playing for Star when I come to visit her."

"Do you mind me asking what happened to her?" she said softly. "You can say no. I know you barely know me."

I wanted to tell her that I knew more about her than she even realized. And it wasn't because I'd had access to her medical chart for a week and a half. I'd never have abused my position like that. It was just because I'd been paying that much attention. But the fact was, I needed to tell her about Candace, and she'd just opened the door for that conversation.

"She and my fiancée, Candace, were hit by a semitruck driver who fell asleep at the wheel about a year ago. Candace was killed on impact, and it's nothing short of a miracle that Star survived. Among a plethora of other things, she suffered a massive spinal cord injury and was told by numerous doctors and therapists that she'd probably never walk again. But she regained feeling in her legs about two months later, and it's been a long, slow road, but she's learning how to walk again."

"Oh, my God," she gasped quietly. "Lennon...I...shit, I suck at stuff like this. I wish knew what to say other than I'm *so* sorry.

About your fiancée, and about Star."

I gave her a sad smile as I took one of her hands and brought it up to my lips for a kiss. "You don't have to say anything. I told you earlier that you woke up something inside me that I thought was dead, and I need you to know I meant every word of it. I was numb. Frozen. Just going through the motions. But from the second I met you, you captivated me, mind, body, and soul. I still can't explain how I felt so much so fast, but I can't ignore it. Not when you've made me *feel* again. And now I'm just praying you feel the same way."

Hope wiped a few tears off her cheeks and chuckled weakly. "You want the truth?"

"Always," I said earnestly.

Her face blazed crimson as she spoke. "You had me at, 'I brought you a sandwich.'"

I laughed, then leaned in for another kiss. It was slow. Sweet. Unhurried. And when *she* was the one to tentatively swipe at my bottom lip, my heart filled to overflowing. I happily opened for her, groaning as our tongues met and began to twist and turn around each other. Tasting. Exploring. Savoring.

I'd *never* been kissed like this before. Ever. And I hoped like hell that this was just the beginning. That this was the first of an infinite number of moments that would leave a permanent mark on my soul.

"Okay, enough with the heavy," I murmured when I finally had to pull back for breath. "Can I play a song for you? Or two?"

She grinned. "I'd love that."

I went to grab my guitar case from where I'd left it next to the door, shut the door so we wouldn't disturb the other patients, and then did some quick tuning before sitting back on the bed. It only took me a second to figure out what to play for her, and surprisingly, it *wasn't* a Rob Thomas song. I'd play "Unwell" for her some other time and tell her how that song was pretty much responsible for bringing us together, but I was trying to *lift* the mood right now, not bring it back down.

So, instead, I started to play "Waiting for Superman." The song that had been playing when she'd told me she didn't think she'd get her own happily ever after. And when I sang the line about a girl being locked up inside her apartment, I realized it was absolutely perfect for her.

"That's one of my favorite songs," Hope chuckled when I was done singing. "I love Chris Daughtry. I'm such a dork. My Spotify playlist is mostly dad rock."

"Nothing wrong with that. Dad rock is my jam," I teased. "But you know what I think about when I hear that song now?"

She shook her head. "What?"

"I think about your second day in the hospital. This song was playing on your computer when I walked in, and I asked what you were working on. When you told me you wrote romance novels, you said you did it because you needed to live vicariously through your characters. Because you didn't think you'd ever get your own happily ever after."

"Oh, my God," she groaned quietly, burying her face in her hands. "I can't believe you remember that."

Peeling her hands away from her face, I tilted her chin up so she'd look at me. "I remember every single second I've spent with you, Hope. And I absolutely remember wanting to tell you right then and there that you'd get a happy ending, and that I wanted to be the one to give it to you. So, will you let me?"

She beamed at me with a hopeful smile before uttering one simple word that filled me with so much joy, I thought I might burst.

"Yes."

fifteen

hope

A smile that could have lit up an entire concert hall spread across Lennon's face, and he leaned down and captured my lips again in a kiss that I could feel all the way down to the very core of my being. A kiss that was soft and tender, yet burned me from the inside out, searching out all the miniscule pieces of my broken soul and soldering them back together.

I still didn't understand what the hell was happening, but somewhere between kissing me senseless and playing one of my favorite songs and telling me he wanted to give me a happily ever after, he'd managed to convince me not to care. Not to sit here overanalyzing it. Because something about this – about *him* – just felt incredibly *right*. Like coming home to a warm fireplace and a mug of hot cocoa after being stuck in a blizzard for days.

As my lips parted on a sigh, he took that opportunity to slip his tongue into my mouth, groaning quietly as I started to let my tongue twist and tangle with his. I let out a whimper as I raised an arm to curl it around his back, while my other hand made its way to his cheek in an attempt to keep his mouth right where it was. He let a hand skim across my stomach before sliding it upward and under my shoulder, pressing his body against mine as he continued to kiss me like a starving man at a banquet.

When I finally had to tear my mouth from his, gulping in lungfuls of air, he just moved his lips to my jawline, trailing kisses down toward my neck. And when he reached my pulse point and pulled my skin into his mouth, sucking softly, I let out an embarrassingly loud moan as I did my damndest to squeeze my legs together to relieve the ache between them. An ache that I hadn't felt in longer than I cared to admit.

An ache that made me feel...*human* again. Deliciously so.

"Oh, my God," I gasped as he grazed his teeth over my neck.

"Fuck, beautiful," he whispered, crashing his lips to mine again. "Those sounds you're making... I don't think you realize how much I wish we weren't in a hospital room right now."

"That makes two of us. I...I almost forgot...what it feels like to...to..." I trailed off, unable to finish that sentence.

I couldn't admit to this perfect specimen of a man that I couldn't remember the last time I'd had an orgasm. That I couldn't even remember the last time I'd *wanted* to have one because until very recently, the only sensation in my body had been debilitating agony.

Lennon pulled back to gaze into my eyes, looking like he was debating something, before glancing at the closed door and then at me again. Then his mouth was back on mine, kissing me breathless as he trailed his hand down my side and let it rest on my hip.

"Can you be quiet, phoenix?" he murmured against my lips.

Oh, my God. That endearment. It was everything. So cheesy because of where it came from, but at the same time, so sweet.

So…us.

"What?" I asked, realizing I had no idea what he'd just asked me because all I'd been able to focus on was him calling me *phoenix*.

"I want to help you remember, beautiful. *So* fucking bad. But I need you to be quiet for me so no one comes in. Can you do that?"

I was pretty sure my eyes got as big as dinner plates. He… he wanted to…

Now? *Here?!*

Lennon chuckled and brushed a kiss on my lips as he toyed with the hem of the pajama shorts I'd *finally* been able to fit my leg into again.

"I need your words, phoenix. Can I touch you?" he whispered, his warm breath washing over me and making my head fuzzy.

At least that was the explanation I was going with, because that was the only possible reason for the next word that came out of my mouth.

"Please," I practically groaned.

He grinned and kissed me again as he slipped his hand into my shorts and slid it through the curls I hadn't been able to shave in at least a year. I parted my legs as much as I could, praying it was wide enough to let him finish what he'd started.

And then his finger was trailing over my slit, torturously light and slow, making every nerve ending in my body stand on high alert. I bit my lip as a whimper escaped me, determined to obey him and stay quiet.

"Lennon," I breathed. "Please. I…I need…"

As he pressed two fingers between my folds, finding my clit and starting to rub, he swallowed my quiet moan in a kiss.

"Shit, phoenix, you're soaked. I love that," he murmured against my lips, gliding his fingers down along either side of the swollen nub before starting to rub a little harder.

His hand left my clit, and I whimpered from the loss of the heavenly friction…until he gently guided my legs a little further apart and slid one finger inside me, slowly pumping it in and out. And before I could stop myself, I moaned in sheer ecstasy.

Lennon captured my lips, drinking down the sounds I was making, as he added another finger. And *fuck*...

It had been so long since I'd been touched like this. Since anyone – or any*thing* – had been inside me. Just two of his fingers made me feel so full, and the way he was fucking me with them was absolute perfection. Swift and deep, but at the same time, so gentle and caring.

"You don't know how much I wish I could hear those sounds," he rasped as he started to rub circles over my clit with his thumb while his fingers curled inside me, brushing against that sweet spot that no one else had ever been able to find. "I can't wait until we're alone and you don't have to hold back."

"Oh, God," I whimpered quietly, biting my lip as I started to buck my hips against his hand, chasing my release with reckless abandon. "Don't stop. *Please* don't stop."

"Wouldn't dream of it," he said quietly as he worked a third finger inside me, filling me to overflowing. "That's it, beautiful. Ride my hand. Take what you need."

"Fuck," I groaned softly as he started plunging his fingers in and out of me, hard and fast. "I...fuck, Lennon!"

Thank God, he didn't stop, despite how loud I'd just been. Instead, he swallowed my cries in a searing kiss while pressing his thumb down harder, making me tremble as molten lava started to flow through my veins, the telltale sign of my impending release.

"Come for me, phoenix," he whispered. "Let go. I promise I'll catch you."

And with the next thrust, I did. I gripped his neck and pulled him back down, crashing my lips to his as my entire world shattered around me. He didn't stop until I went limp under him, panting like I'd just run a marathon. Pulling back as he slipped his hand out of my shorts, he gave me one of those kind, heartwarmingly sincere smiles I'd grown to love so much, looking at me like I'd just made his whole life.

…Right before wiping the tears off my cheeks with his dry thumb.

I hadn't even realized I was crying. But for the first time in a long time, these tears weren't heartache or pain. They were tears of absolute, pure joy. Because he'd given me something I'd never thought I would get again. He'd made me feel human.

No, he'd made me feel like *a woman*.

lennon

"You okay, beautiful?" I asked quietly, cupping Hope's cheek in my hand as I swiped at another tear on her face.

"I'm perfect," she breathed, so soft it was barely audible. "That was…you were… These are good tears, I promise."

I chuckled as I leaned down to brush my lips against her swollen ones. "Good. I'll be right back."

She nodded quickly. "Okay."

Pressing a featherlight kiss to her forehead, I stood and walked into the bathroom to wash my hands. My head was spinning as I wondered who the hell I was and what I'd done with Lennon McCartney, the healthcare professional. The man who knew a nurse or tech could have walked in on us at any moment and gotten a glimpse at her in the throes of passion as I'd brought her to the edge of sanity and then caught her as she tumbled over the cliff in a freefall. The way only *I* was supposed to see her.

But hearing her say that she didn't even remember what being with a man felt like…it broke my heart. And fuck, it had just felt *right* – necessary, even – to seize the moment. Despite the fact that my cock was currently throbbing, begging for the release I wouldn't let myself have. Not until Hope was back at home and I was deep inside her, showing her what I didn't have the words to express out loud.

Because no part of this had been about me. It was all about her. About reminding her that she was so much more than this godawful condition that had stolen the last several years of her life from her. That she was a human being and she was allowed to want things. To feel things other than pain. Like pleasure. And love.

Hope blushed crimson and averted her eyes when I walked out of the bathroom and sat back down on the bed next to her.

"Nope," I chuckled, gently turning her head so she'd look at me, then pressing a kiss to her lips. "None of that, phoenix. You don't have a single thing to be ashamed of. That was one of the best moments of my entire life. Despite how dumb it was of me to start it."

If it was possible, her cheeks got even redder as she chucked nervously. "Phoenix? Really?"

I snorted. Because, yeah, I knew that was the character Sydney Bristow's code name in seasons four and five of *Alias*. But honestly, it was sort of perfect for Hope too.

"Yes, really. Because after everything you've been through, you're still here. Still fighting. Just like a phoenix rising from the ashes."

Hope swallowed hard as a tear glistened in the corner of her eye before starting to trail down her cheek. I swiped it away with my thumb, then bent down to kiss her forehead.

"Damn it," she chuckled, sniffling a little. "Stop making me cry. It feels like all I've done is cry lately."

"That's okay," I assured her. "You're allowed to cry. Everything you've dealt with lately...hell, if the tables were turned, I wouldn't be handling it with near as much strength and courage and grace as you are. It's absolutely okay not to be okay. Just know I'm not going anywhere. I'm here, every step of the way. For whatever you need."

"Such as a mind-blowing orgasm in a hospital room, apparently," she snickered.

I laughed. "Happy to be of service."

Then I stole our hundredth kiss today. Because now that I was allowed to kiss her, I couldn't get enough. I'd *never* get enough of her.

"But the next time I make you come, it's going to be in my mouth," I whispered into her ear, grazing my teeth against her earlobe. "And you're going to be able to scream at the top of your lungs."

sixteen

lennon
five days later

ME

Hey, beautiful. How's your day?

I sat down on a bench outside the hospital, enjoying the daylight for a few precious moments before I had to head in to work, as I waited for Hope's reply.

We'd been texting every day since the day she'd agreed to give us a try, but I'd only gotten to spend a grand total of five minutes with her in person since then. The one time I'd made it to the rehab center to see her and Star this week, she'd been in the middle of physical therapy, so I'd only briefly gotten to stop by and say hello.

It was a little stupid how much I missed her. Texting was

better than nothing, but the feeling I got when I was actually in the same room with her...there was nothing else like it.

My phone buzzed with a response.

HOPE

Better now. 😌

PT SUUUUCKED today. I swear Sean was trying to kill me with how many times he made me go up and down the stairs. 😵‍💫😵‍💫😵‍💫

I smiled as I typed my response.

ME

Do you realize how amazing it is that you're able to go up and down stairs now, though? I'm proud of you, phoenix. You've come so far in just two and a half weeks. 🖤

Yeah, I was the guy who used heart emojis in his texts – when it was warranted, and this was definitely a situation that called for it.

HOPE

Bashful from Snow White "Aww shucks" GIF

ME

I mean it, beautiful. A lot of people would have given up a long time ago, but you haven't. Not once.

HOPE

I can't give up. I want my life back. At least some of it.

ME

I know. And I'll do anything I can to help you reclaim it. You know that, right?

HOPE

I know. And I appreciate it more than you know. Speaking of which…I was actually just about to text you when I got your message. The doctor came to see me a little while ago and she told me I get to go home tomorrow!

Which means I'll be home when Noah and Peyton get here in two days. 😄

ME

That's amazing!!! 😺😺😺

Do you know what time you're getting discharged?

HOPE

Around eleven, I think. Had to be early because April's working the night shift and she's driving me home. And she has to bring the fluffballs back to my place too. I miss them something fierce.

She was seriously getting a ride in April's Ford Fiesta? There was no way she'd be comfortable in that. She wouldn't be able to stretch her leg out at all.

But I also knew hospitals were notoriously horrible about arranging for transport when patients were ready to be discharged, so I couldn't say I was surprised. I'd bought something for her that would be helpful for this occasion, though – something April had mentioned that she sorely needed and couldn't afford – and I also had a much more comfortable Ford Escape.

ME

How would you feel about letting me be your chauffeur instead? Then April just has to worry about Sydney and Vaughn. Who I can't wait to meet BTW.

HOPE

I don't want to make you come all the way out here. My complex is on the complete opposite end of town.

ME

You realize there's nothing I wouldn't do for you, right? And I'll never say no to spending time with you, no matter what.

HOPE

If you're sure, I'd love that. You know, in case I need some man muscle to help me get up the sixteen stairs to my apartment.

Sixteen stairs? No wonder she was homebound. Even if she was able to drive – which I knew she hadn't been able to do for a while – she couldn't even get to the parking lot of her own apartment complex without it being a whole-ass production.

And as I realized that, a thought began to take root in my mind. Something that, on the surface, seemed completely harebrained and illogical, but at the same time felt overwhelmingly right. Because maybe, just maybe, it might help her reclaim some of her independence.

But this wasn't the time to talk to her about it. That was a conversation we needed to have in person, not over text. So I responded with humor instead.

ME

That's what I'm here for. Muscle Man Lennon at your service. 💪😊

HOPE

ME

Maybe I can cook you dinner tomorrow night too? Since you can't actually go out on a date, I want to bring the date to you. And I'm off the next couple of days after tonight.

HOPE

Aww! I'd love that! 😊

ME

What am I making? Since you've been stuck eating shitty hospital food for almost three weeks, you get to pick.

HOPE

I'm not picky. ANYTHING is better than the food at this place.

Translation: she didn't want to tell me what she wanted because it wasn't something like flavorless steamed vegetables with slimy tofu.

That was another thing we were going to have to work on. Helping her repair her relationship with food and taking away her shame every time she took a bite of something that wasn't celery. I knew it'd take a while and it'd be a process, but we'd get there. And it would start tomorrow night. With me reminding her that food – *all* food – was meant to be enjoyed.

"Hey, Lennon," came April's voice, distracting me from the conversation.

I looked up to find her grinning at me.

"Texting with Hope?" she guessed.

I chuckled as I stood up. "Yep. She told me she gets to go home tomorrow."

"Yep, she does," she sighed as we walked toward the hospital.

Turning to look at her, I raised an eyebrow. "You sound *thrilled*."

"Oh, my God, of course I am!" she said quickly. "I'm *so* glad she's gotten better enough to go home. And her social worker is trying to find a home health agency that will take her Medicare advantage plan so she can continue with the lymphedema therapy at home for a while too, which is amazing. It's just gonna be a long day, and my car's gonna get a workout too."

"Actually, I think I can help with that," I told her. "I'm going to give her a ride home. I think my Escape will be a lot more comfortable for her than your Fiesta. So you just have to worry about bringing the cats back to her place."

"Hallelujah, thank you Jesus," she practically groaned, pressing the call button for the elevator. "You're a lifesaver! I'll make us lunch too and have it ready when you get there."

Aha! Food! *This* was how I could figure out what to make for dinner tomorrow. I guessed it paid to work with my girlfriend's best friend.

"Speaking of food…I'm cooking us dinner tomorrow night since I've got the next couple of nights off. I want to have a stay-in date with her. But I have no idea what to make."

"Because she won't tell you," April finished for me, shaking her head and rolling her eyes. "Figures. Well, she *loves* Italian food. Gnocchi is one of her most favorite things ever. Especially with pesto. Maybe some grilled chicken or shrimp for protein, and carrots or broccoli for a veggie. But roast the veggies, don't steam them. She's not a fan of soggy vegetables."

That was easily doable. There was a world market close to where I lived that I knew carried a couple of different flavors of gnocchi because I'd seen it there and had always wanted to try it. I'd just have to figure out how to cook it. Maybe Hope could help me with that if I made sure there was a comfortable chair in the kitchen for her to sit on while I worked.

"Oh, and if you want to do dessert, her absolute favorite treat is carrot cake. Or tiramisu if you want to stick with the Italian theme."

"That sounds perfect. Thanks. And now I'm hungry," I laughed as the elevator doors closed behind us.

"You're welcome," she giggled. "But this is the part where I tell you that I like you, but if you break my bestie's heart, I'll break your face. Capisce?"

I snorted. "Noted. And I promise I won't. I know this is still new, but I'm in it for the long haul. I'm not going anywhere, and I'll do whatever I can to make her life easier. She's been through enough already."

April smiled. "You know, as much as I hate the way you and Hope met, I'm *so* glad you did. You deserve each other, and you're both happier than I've seen you in a long time. The universe just has a shitty way of working its magic sometimes."

That made me grin. I could tell April was protective of her friend, which I was glad for, so to get her seal of approval on my budding relationship with Hope meant everything to me.

"I hate the way we met too," I told her. "But even if this hadn't happened, I know we would have crossed paths eventually. Because meeting her…it couldn't have been anything other than fate."

seventeen

hope

Why the hell was I so nervous?

I was beyond ready to go home. My wounds had healed, I could get out of bed and even walk a little now, and my social worker had found a home health agency for me so I could continue my lymphedema therapy from the comfort of my own home. So why did the thought of leaving scare me so much?

A knock sounded on my doorframe, and I looked over expecting my nurse, Van, to walk in. But it wasn't her.

It was Lennon…half an hour early, pushing a folded-up wheelchair that looked much bigger – and infinitely more comfortable – than the one the rehab center had loaned me. And it also had an elevated leg rest so I could prop my leg up rather than have to try to keep it on the stupid little footrest while squeezing my legs together.

Why the heck had the hospital made me use the wheelchair I'd been using for the past week if they had this kind of chair available? That kind of pissed me off.

"Hey," I murmured. "You're early."

"I know," he chuckled as he parked the chair a couple of feet away from the bed and unfolded it. "But I figured you might need some help getting your stuff packed up."

Then he walked over and bent down to kiss me while sliding an arm under my shoulders as our lips and tongues danced effortlessly together. I whimpered slightly as all the memories about the last time he'd been in this room flooded back. The way he'd touched me. The way he'd kissed me. The way he'd made my body come alive for the first time in years.

God, I couldn't wait for tonight. When we'd finally be completely alone.

But at the same time, I was nervous as hell for it. It had been so long since I'd been on a date – stay-in or otherwise – and I honestly didn't know how I was supposed to act. Despite the fact that I wrote this kind of stuff for a living. And if things did start to get physical, I honestly wasn't sure if I'd be able to do much more than make out with him. I didn't know if my back and leg would allow me to have sex, no matter how much I wanted to.

And dear Lord, did I want to. It was almost all I could think about. Particularly the whispered promise he'd made me about the next time he would make me come.

"Missed you, phoenix," he whispered against my lips before pecking my nose and tucking some hair behind my ear.

"I missed you too," I admitted as my cheeks heated. "You didn't have to get a wheelchair from downstairs. I've still got the one they loaned me up here. Though I'm a little upset they gave me the one I've been using for the past week when they had that one available instead."

Lennon flashed me a ten-thousand-megawatt smile. "This isn't the hospital's wheelchair. It's yours."

Wait, what?

"I don't have—"

"You do now," he chuckled. "Surprise, beautiful."

I was sure I looked like an old-school *Looney Tunes* character – eyes bugged out, jaw on the floor, the whole nine yards.

I'd tried a couple of different times to get my insurance to cover a wheelchair so I could go out without having to worry about how many steps would be between my car and the next place I could sit down and rest. Because lugging around an extra hundred pounds of dead weight with every step I took? It was brutal. Not only did it hurt my leg, but it *killed* my back too – which was already a mess, thanks to degenerative disc disease.

But because I lived in a second-floor walk-up apartment, they'd always denied it, saying that if I was able to get up and down stairs, a wheelchair wasn't a medical necessity. And then I'd looked into costs to purchase one out of pocket, and for a bariatric wheelchair like I needed...well, living on SSDI, I couldn't afford it.

And now a man I'd known for less than a month was just *giving* me one? And one that might as well have been custom-made for my needs, at that.

Oh, God. Please *don't tell me it was custom-made.*

Okay, so Lennon wasn't just any man. He was...my boyfriend? Maybe? Sort of? We'd sort of skipped over the part where we put a label on whatever it was we were doing. More than a friend, anyway. But still. This wasn't a box of chocolates or a bouquet of flowers. That chair must have cost him at least four hundred dollars. Probably closer to six hundred.

"I...you...what?" I stammered, at a complete loss for words.

"I was talking to April a few days ago, and she told me your insurance wouldn't cover a wheelchair since you live in a walk-up apartment building. Which is the biggest crock of shit I've ever heard, by the way. Anyway, I thought maybe with this chair, you might be able to get out of the house every now and then. With me, or even with April and Peyton. I know it'll still be hard and it won't be an all-the-time thing, but I just wanted to do something to help you find your new normal and make your life a little easier."

Damn it, Hope. Don't cry. Do not *cry. You can't cry every time someone does something nice for you. Get it together.*

Nope, it was useless. I couldn't even swallow the lump in my throat before tears were trickling out of my eyes. For the fucking zillionth time in the past three weeks.

But Lennon wasn't fazed. Not even a little bit. He just sat down next to me on the bed and wiped them away before brushing a kiss over my lips. But a little whisper of a kiss wasn't nearly enough. Especially since I'd apparently forgotten how to speak.

So I pulled him back in and poured all of the shock, awe, confusion, gratitude, and love – every single emotion that was putting my mind into overdrive – into the kiss I gave him. I didn't come up for air until my lungs were burning and begging me to take a breath.

"I don't know what to say," I sniffled. "Other than thank you. So much."

"Anything for you, phoenix," he murmured. "Now let's get you packed up so we can get out of here."

My stomach started to twist into a knot and bile rose in my throat when Lennon parked my wheelchair right at the bottom of the stairs. I'd been preparing for this moment, walking back up the stairs to my apartment, for the past week, and I had thought I was ready for it.

But now, sitting here at the bottom of the first of two eight-step flights of stairs, I was terrified. What if I couldn't do it? What if my leg gave out and I collapsed? What if I tripped over my own two feet and face-planted on one of these concrete steps? What if—

"Breathe with me, Hope," Lennon murmured as he knelt in front of me, gliding one hand up the side of my good leg while using the other to tilt my chin toward him. "Slow, deep breath in."

He coached me through at least ten controlled breaths before the knot in my stomach even started to loosen, but it was still just sitting there like a bowling ball, refusing to dissipate completely.

Had it really been that obvious how scared I was of these stupid stairs? Or did he just know me that well already?

"I'm right here with you, phoenix," he said softly. "I won't let you fall. And you can go as slow as you need to. Just focus on getting up the first set of steps, and then we'll take a break before we do the next one. Okay?"

I nodded, still too nervous to speak.

Rising halfway, he whispered a kiss over my lips. And somehow *that* was what made the knot uncurl, leaving behind a swarm of butterflies instead.

"You ready for me to put the leg rests down?" he asked, pulling back to look me in the eyes.

"No," I admitted. "But I can't just sit here all day."

"You can sit here as long as you need, beautiful. But remember, your best friend and your fur babies are at the top of those stairs, and they can't wait to see you."

"April and Vaughn, maybe. Sydney will probably be mad at me for a few days before she gives me snuggles." I snorted. "She's an asshole, but I love her. Okay, let's do this."

Lennon chuckled. "Okay. I'm right here. I'm not going to let you get hurt."

I nodded, and he gently lowered the elevated leg rest and helped me get my bad leg down, then pushed it off to the side before swinging the other leg rest out of the way so I could stand without any obstructions. My legs shook as I raised myself out of the chair, but I pushed through it and was rewarded with a kiss when I stood to my full height.

Hobbling the few steps to the stairs, I grasped the handrail and used my good leg to step onto the first stair, dragging my bad leg up behind me. And it wasn't nearly as bad as I'd been afraid of. In less than a minute, I scaled the first flight of stairs, discovering that keeping the momentum going made it easier. But when I reached the first platform halfway up, I turned and carefully lowered myself onto the second flight of stairs to take a quick break.

"You did great, phoenix," came Lennon's encouraging voice as he knelt in front of me and stole a quick kiss. "Rest as long as you need to, but just remember that the longer you wait, the harder it'll be to get going again."

I took a minute to catch my breath, then he helped me back to my feet and I scaled the second flight of stairs only slightly slower than I'd done the first one. And then I was standing right in front of my apartment door. I dug in my purse for my key and unlocked the door, cautiously pushing it open to make sure the cats wouldn't run out.

"Welcome home!" April squealed as she sprang up from the couch.

I shot her an exhausted smile. "Thanks. Are the cats gonna get out if I open this door the rest of the way?"

"Nope, you're safe. I put them in the bedroom when I heard you coming up the stairs. Now get in here so I can hug you!"

That was when realized I still had to step up into my apartment, where there was nothing for me to hold onto for leverage. But Lennon seemed to realize that all by himself, because he stepped inside, then held out his hands to help me.

Once I was safely inside the apartment, he kissed my forehead. "You did amazing, phoenix. You okay if I go grab your bags and chair?"

I nodded. "Thanks. For everything."

He flashed me one of those smiles that made my insides turn to goo and planted a soft, lingering kiss on my lips. "Anything for you. I'll be back in a few."

As he walked back out the door, shutting it behind him, I made my way to the couch. And once I was comfortably settled and had my feet up, April opened the bedroom door before jumping onto the couch next to me and flinging her arms around my neck. I laughed and returned the hug.

"Did you…have this couch cleaned?" I asked, realizing it no longer had lymphatic fluid stains all over it.

"Yep," she chuckled. "I couldn't let you come home to a dirty, stained couch, so I rented a steam-cleaner and did it a few days ago. I also did all your laundry for you, which is in a couple of baskets in the bedroom, and cleaned out and restocked your fridge. Oh, and I made a *huge* batch of that grape tomato, orzo, and feta salad you love so much. Figured we could have it with some sandwiches today and tomorrow. I called Noah and made sure Peyton didn't have any allergies."

"Thank you," I mumbled, giving her another squeeze. "So much."

"What are friends for?" she said with a smile.

Vaughn jumped up on my chest and started kneading at my shoulder, and I sniffled a little as I turned my attention to him.

"Hey, buddy," I murmured, scratching behind his ears and chuckling when he leaned his whole body into my hand. "Hi. I love you too. I missed you so much."

Purring loudly, he crouched on my chest, then curled his paws under his body in a loafing position. Sydney, on the other hand, just looked at me from her spot on the floor, like she couldn't quite believe I was really here.

"Come here, sweet girl," I cooed, patting the other side of my chest. "I missed you too."

But she just curled up on the floor right next to the couch. Then again, for Sydney, that was pretty much the equivalent of rolling out the red carpet.

"She's been so moody the entire time you've been gone," April snickered. "But then again, she's pretty much always moody."

I snorted and loved on Vaughn a little more. "True story. *This* one's the attention whore."

"So, talk to me about tonight. Are you excited? Nervous? Scared?"

"D. All of the above," I admitted. "I'm just...I'm worried that if things start to head in the direction I think they're going to, I won't be able to follow through. I don't want to lead him on and then end up disappointing him if my leg and back decide they hate me."

"You definitely *don't* have to worry about that. I've worked with Lennon for years. He's one of the best friends I've made at the hospital. And after..." She trailed off, like she wasn't sure if she should say more.

Because she didn't know if I knew.

"Candace," I finished for her. "He told me about the accident. I wanted to meet Star while I was at the rehab center, but our therapy schedules didn't let it happen. I think we actually had the same physical therapist."

"I went to high school with her. She's a total sweetheart. Anyway, my point in bringing that up was to say that he knows exactly what he's signing up for. Hell, he's seen you at your absolute lowest. And the fact that he's even decided he wants to explore what the two of you have after what happened means that he's serious about you. He won't be disappointed if you have to put the brakes on because your body isn't up for sex yet. He'll be glad that you told him because I *know* that the last thing he'd ever want is for you to push yourself to do something that'll end up hurting you."

I really hoped she was right. But more than that, I hoped she didn't *have* to be right.

Because I hoped my leg would cooperate for once in my damn life and let me make love to the man who had brought me back into the light after I'd spent years in the darkness.

"He told me he's staying to have lunch with us, and then he has to go grocery shopping for our date tonight. Do you think you could stay after he leaves and help me with a shower and picking out something niceish to wear?" I asked sheepishly. "Even though we're not going anywhere, I still want to put in a little effort."

April grinned. "Absolutely."

eighteen

lennon

Hope couldn't stay here.

I'd been thinking that ever since she'd told me how many steps there were to get up to her unit, but now that I'd seen this complex in person? Nope. Just nope. These stairs were a beast even for someone in perfect health. Not to mention, the entire building looked run-down and definitely was *not* wheelchair accessible.

I needed to get her out of here. The sooner, the better. I knew we'd only just met and that we'd been a couple for a grand total of six days, but this wasn't just about the way I felt. This was about her safety and getting her into a handicap-accessible living space…which I had, since I was living in my grandparents' old house that I'd inherited when they died. She needed to be in a space where she could thrive and figure out what her new normal was, with someone who loved and supported her unconditionally.

The look on her face when she realized that I'd bought her a wheelchair, the way she'd kissed me…God, I honestly didn't know whether to be overjoyed or heartbroken. Her entire life was a constant battle to do even the simplest things – things most people just took for granted – and it shouldn't have been that way.

Using the key she'd given me, I unlocked her apartment door and walked inside with two reusable grocery bags full of food and my guitar, plus a comfortable oversized lawn chair in its canvas bag slung across my back so she could sit in the kitchen and we could talk while I cooked.

I saw a flash of white as Sydney dashed into the bedroom, and Hope snorted a laugh as she paused the episode of *Alias* she was watching and turned to me, smiling so big it could have lit up the entire town. And as I took in the sage-green three-quarter-length dress she was wearing and her slightly damp hair – which meant she'd done her best to dress up for tonight, since she'd essentially been wearing pajamas when she left the rehab center – my heart somersaulted in my chest.

This was a sight I could get used to coming home to.

"Oh, my God. What did you *do*?" she chuckled. "That's an obscene amount of groceries. And is that…a lawn chair?"

Grinning, I set my guitar case next to the couch, then walked over to where she was sitting, bending down for a slow, lingering kiss. "Yes, it is a lawn chair. I wanted to be able to talk to you while I cooked, so I grabbed a comfortable chair for you. And I thought maybe I could set up one of those TV trays and you could help me with some of the prep work if you're up for it."

Not that I was trying to make her work tonight, but I got the feeling it had been a while since she'd felt useful, so I wanted to give her the option.

"I'd love to help," she said, beaming up at me like I'd just made her entire year.

"Okay. Let me go put these groceries down and get this chair set up for you. I don't want you walking on that linoleum floor without me."

She snorted. "Fair. It'd kinda put a damper on the evening if I ate it on the slippery kitchen floor."

It only took a minute to get the chair set up and her situated. Then I grabbed a wooden TV tray off the rack in the living room and set it up in front of her. Pulling a wooden cutting board I'd grabbed from home out of the bag, I set that and a knife in front of her before retrieving the rainbow carrots I'd bought from a local farmer's market this afternoon.

"Oh, my God. These look *amazing*," she gushed.

"Right? I struck gold at the farmer's market," I agreed. "We're roasting these with some olive oil, salt, and pepper, so just chop off the tops and cut them into quarters. Do you have another cutting board by chance?"

"Yep. Cabinet right next to the oven. Pots and pans are there too. And if we need a cooking sheet for the carrots, that's in the drawer under the oven."

"That was going to be my next question," I chuckled. "But first…are you a wine drinker? I got a bottle of pinot grigio."

"Cupboard to the right of the sink," she informed me. "And I love white wine. Red, not so much. Don't ask me why. Oh, and the corkscrew is in the drawer next to the stove. Along with a bunch of other random shit."

I retrieved two wine glasses and popped open the bottle of wine, pouring us each a glass before pulling the carrot cake I'd bought out of the second bag and finding a place for it in the fridge. When I looked over at Hope, her eyes were bugging out of her head, like she couldn't believe I'd feed her cake.

"Okay, please tell me you know how to cook gnocchi," I said as I pulled the two packages I'd bought out. "Because I've never even had it before, let alone cooked it."

"You…you got all my favorites," she murmured, so quietly I almost didn't hear her.

"I might have had a little help," I admitted.

When she continued to stare wide-eyed at me, like she was in complete shock, I decided I needed to address the elephant in the room. Not just because I didn't want tonight to be awkward, but because she needed to understand that I would *never* shame her for her food choices.

Kneeling next to her chair, I put a hand under her chin, gently turning her head toward me. But she kept her eyes downcast.

"Look at me, beautiful," I implored her. "Please."

After hesitating for a second, she slowly raised her eyes to meet mine, a mixture of hesitation, nerves, and fear swimming in them.

"You *never* have to be ashamed about what you're eating with me," I told her. "Ever. Food is meant to be enjoyed. *All* food. It's about balance, not about denying yourself the things you love."

"Then why has every doctor I've ever had tried to tell me—"

"Because they're a bunch of misogynistic, fatphobic asshats," I cut her off. "But all diet culture does is put unrealistic expectations on people and set them up for failure in the long run. It's normal and healthy to treat yourself every now and then. And tonight's a special occasion. It's our first date *and* your first night at home after being in the hospital for almost three weeks. Yeah, you might need a little extra insulin since we're having wine and cake and a carb-heavy meal, but that's what it's there for."

Hope took a shaky breath, still seeming like she couldn't believe what she was hearing. "If you say so."

"I do say so. Besides, I've got plans for how to burn some of those calories later," I said with a wink. "So put everything you've been told out of your head tonight and just enjoy every second *and* every bite. Got it?"

Her face flushed crimson as she let out a nervous chuckle. "Got it."

"Good." I brushed my lips over hers as I stood back up. "So, do I need to Google how to cook the gnocchi, or can you help me out?"

"Nope, no Googling required," she said as she took a sip of wine. "It's actually easier than pasta because there's no guesswork involved. Just boil a pot of water and dump it in. When it floats, it's done."

nineteen

hope

Note: The song "Hold on Forever" by Rob Thomas plays a significant role in this chapter. If you don't know it, I highly recommend listening to it to get the full effect.

I was *stuffed.*

I'd honestly forgotten how filling gnocchi with pesto cream sauce was. Add to that the roasted rainbow carrots and some perfectly seasoned grilled chicken, plus the slice of carrot cake I'd eaten, and it felt like I'd just consumed Thanksgiving dinner.

But it was worth it. I couldn't even remember the last time I'd had a meal that good, even though I was a little ashamed of the fact that I'd all but licked my plate clean. I could have saved some of it and had it for dinner tomorrow. Probably should have. But Lennon had polished off his plate too, telling me that he'd discovered a new favorite food. The groan he'd emitted when he took his first bite of gnocchi had made me want to say screw the food and have *him* for dinner instead.

"So, where'd you learn to cook like that?" I asked as he walked back into the living room after rinsing off the dishes and loading them in the dishwasher.

"My mom," he said, grabbing his guitar case and sitting down next to me. "She owns The Farmhouse Eatery and still does most of the cooking herself, even though she has other chefs on the payroll."

"No way," I gasped. "I love that place. I used to go there all the time."

"Well, I know what I'm doing for date number two, then. I'll just get my mom to cater it."

"I'd love that." I grinned as I gestured to his guitar. "So, now that you've fed me, you're planning to serenade me?"

Lennon snorted. "Something like that."

Then he took a deep breath, averting his eyes like he was afraid to say whatever was on his mind. After a few seconds, he looked up at me.

"The day after I met you, I went to visit Star," he sighed. "And for the first time since the accident, I brought my guitar with me. At first, I was trying to just have some fun with her and play some of her favorite songs. But then she told me to stop closing myself off from what I was feeling and to play something real. She thought she was trying to get me to work through some of my emotions about the accident, but the truth was, everything I was feeling that day was about you. I couldn't stop thinking about you. About the pain you were in, about how alone and scared you must have felt, and about how I wanted more than anything to take it all away. Before I even realized it, I was playing one of Candace and I's favorite songs. One that used to remind us to stick together through the good times and the bad. Except every single thought in my head as I played it was about you.

"Then I went to work that night, and you had music playing on your computer as I hooked up your antibiotics. And of all the songs that could have started playing while I was there, it was the same damn song. I don't know if I believe in the supernatural, but I do know how I felt. I could have sworn that she was trying to reach out to me, trying to tell me that it was okay to feel this way about you. That it was okay to move on and let myself be happy. Anyway, since that song is basically responsible for bringing us together, I wanted to play it for you tonight."

Even if he hadn't started to play "Unwell," I wouldn't have had to ask him what song it was. I remembered. I remembered the way he'd frozen right there in the middle of my room, IV tube in hand as his eyes bugged out of his head. I'd assumed it was because I'd just stuck my foot in my mouth up to the knee, but now that I knew the whole story, I couldn't help the fluttering of my heart and the emotions clogging my throat. Not only because of the heartfelt way he was singing, like he meant every single word of it, but also because of the bizarre coincidence.

Because this song? It had pretty much single-handedly gotten me through all the pain and trauma I'd been through since my health had started to decline. What were the chances that of all the songs he'd started singing to express *his* emotions about meeting me for the first time – and of all the songs that had been special to him and Candace – it was this one?

"You want to know something funny?" I let out a watery chuckle. "I swear that's been my theme song for the past couple of years. Since my health took a nosedive."

Lennon gave me a sad smile. "I guessed as much. But it doesn't have to be anymore. Because you're not alone anymore, phoenix. I'm not going anywhere, no matter what. So, I think this Rob Thomas song is a little more appropriate for us."

He started playing one of my absolute favorite songs: "Hold on Forever." And it took everything in me not to completely break down. Knowing about the story behind this song and Marisol Thomas's battle with her own serious health scare, and that Rob had stuck with her through every heart-stopping moment of fear and doubt and pain… God, Lennon couldn't have picked a more perfect song for us. And if that wasn't enough, the way he was looking at me as he sang, like I was the only woman in the whole world, made me melt into a puddle of mush.

By the time he was done playing, I was completely speechless. Lost in the emotions swirling around us, so thick they were palpable. In the way he made me feel seen, understood, and cherished. And in his gaze, which pinned me with such intensity, it took my breath away.

So, instead of opening my mouth and ruining the moment, I just took the guitar out of his hands, set it on the coffee table, and leaned over to kiss him. And the quiet moan that he emitted as he parted his lips and slid his tongue out to meet mine made my heart swell so much, I could have sworn it would burst out of my chest.

"I love you, Hope," he whispered against my lips as his hand palmed my hip, his thumb rubbing circles into my skin. "I think I've loved you since the night I met you."

I wanted so badly to ask him why. Why, out of everyone in the world he could have picked to give the gift of his love to, he'd chosen someone as broken as me. But I couldn't do that. I couldn't spoil the sheer perfection of this night by shattering the bubble he'd so carefully crafted around us. So I went for simplicity instead.

"I fell in love with you that night too," I murmured.

Twenty

lennon

It turned out love at first sight did still exist. Because somehow in the course of three weeks, the incredible woman sitting next to me had become the center of my whole world. And knowing that she felt the same way? God, I couldn't remember the last time I'd been this happy.

Pulling Hope into my arms, I crushed my lips to hers, pouring everything I felt for her into the connection. All the joy, sorrow, love, and…well, hope that had sprung up in me from the second I met her. Drinking down her soft moans like a starving man at a banquet, I kissed her slowly, taking my time and savoring everything about her.

As she tightened her arms around me and shifted, trying unsuccessfully to get closer to me, I started to lower her onto the couch. But almost immediately, her moans and whimpers turned into grunts as she squirmed under me, so I pulled back to look at her.

"Is this okay, beautiful?" I asked, trailing a finger over her cheek.

She nodded and craned her neck to kiss me again. "More than okay. But…can we take this to the bedroom? This couch hates me."

"Absolutely." I smiled and pecked her nose before standing up and holding my hands out to help her to her feet.

Moving slowly – but still at an actual walk rather than the hobbling she'd been doing for the past couple of weeks – she led me into her bedroom, but left the light off as she sat on the bed. I remedied that situation immediately, flicking the switch on before dropping to my knees in front of her and taking her face between my hands.

"Don't hide from me, phoenix," I whispered. "I want to see every inch of the woman I love while I take my time worshiping her."

Before she could say anything, I kissed her hard and deep, wrapping one arm around her waist and pulling her close, relishing in the perfection of her soft curves molding perfectly against me. She wrapped her arms around me, letting her hands wander beneath my shirt collar as our tongues twisted and tangled around each other. And even this simple skin-on-skin contact had every nerve ending in my body zinging like a live wire.

"Can I take this dress off?" I asked against her lips.

Taking a shaky breath, Hope nodded before nudging me backward. I sank back on my heels while she rose to her feet and pulled the dress over her head, leaving her in nothing but a set of white lace lingerie. I swallowed hard as I gazed at her perfect figure. Because she *was* perfect, no matter what her disability had done to her.

Reaching my hand out, I palmed her right hip before letting my hand slide down to caress her ass and then trailing it down over her thigh. I heard her suck in a breath and looked up to find her gazing down at me with a mixture of fear, nerves, and awe… plus a dash of pain.

Because she'd literally *just* gotten home from the hospital today, and like an asshole, I was just making her stand there on her bum leg.

Planting a kiss on her stomach, I moved my hands to her panties, then glanced back up at her for permission. She gave me a wordless nod, so I hooked my fingers into either side and slid the fabric down to the floor, then gave her a gentle nudge toward the bed. When she was seated again, I guided her legs apart and knelt between them, rising slightly to kiss her.

"You're so damn gorgeous," I murmured as I unclasped her bra and slid it down her arms.

"And you're overdressed," she chuckled nervously.

I quickly pulled my shirt over my head and tossed it on the floor. "Better?"

"Much," she said with a quiet snort as she pulled me back in for another kiss.

As I folded my arms around her, holding her close as our mouths moved together effortlessly, a moan rose in my throat at the sheer perfection of feeling her skin against mine with no barriers. But then I noticed the tremors coursing through her body and pulled back, cupping her face in my hands.

"You're shaking like a leaf, phoenix," I said softly. "Talk to me. Is this too much too soon?"

"No," she breathed. "God, no. It's not that. I want this. So much. But I'm nervous. It's been a while since… And I'm scared my body won't let me do this. I'm scared I'll have to stop because I'm nowhere close to a hundred percent right now."

"It's okay if you need to stop," I assured her, brushing a kiss over her lips. "I want you more than my next breath, but I could just keep kissing you all night and be the happiest man on earth. Tonight's about you, not me."

"No, it's not. It's about both of us."

"Well, what *I* want is to make you feel good. As much as you can handle. Which means I need you to be comfortable. So, how can I help with that?"

"I think I need to lie down before my back starts screaming at me," she sighed.

I smiled. "Okay. Then let's get you in bed."

Stealing a quick kiss, I rose to my feet, and Hope turned to lie down. I noticed that she was struggling to get her bad leg up, so I gently lifted it onto the bed, then let her get settled against the pillows while I stripped down to my boxer briefs.

Crawling over her, I kissed her deeply, skimming my hand down her waist and palming her good leg to bend it up. As her arms curled around my shoulders, I felt her trying to bend the other leg, so I pulled back to look at her.

"Do we need to put something under your leg? A pillow or a bunched-up blanket?"

She shook her head. "I'm okay for now. Just need to remember my leg doesn't work the way it used to."

I kissed her nose. "Okay." Then I slid my arm under her shoulders and brought my lips back to hers. "I love you. So much."

That made her smile. "I love you too."

As our mouths met again, I let go of her leg and let my hand wander between her thighs, dipping between her folds and starting to rub her clit.

"Fuck, beautiful, you're soaked," I groaned.

"It's all for you," she breathed as she arched her hips and pressed back against my hand. "Oh, God. That feels so good."

"I'm about to make you feel a whole lot better," I murmured. "I made you a promise last weekend, and I've been dying to keep it. Will you let me? Can I taste you, phoenix?"

She raised her head to kiss me. "You don't have to ask. I'm all yours."

With one more kiss that I only broke when my lungs were screaming and burning for oxygen, I shimmied down the bed, pausing briefly to tug one nipple into my mouth and swirl my tongue over it before trailing my lips over to the other breast and paying the other nipple similar attention. Then I moved down between her legs, settling on my stomach as I lifted her good leg and propped it up on my shoulder while blowing a long breath over her core.

Parting her folds with my fingers, I flicked my tongue over her clit, groaning at the sweet, tangy flavor of her arousal.

"So damn sweet," I mumbled.

Then I dove in headfirst, pulling her clit into my mouth and sucking hard. And the loud moan she emitted? Fucking music to my ears.

"Oh, shit!" she cried.

As I licked, nibbled, and sucked on her swollen bud, spurred on by the steady stream of moans and cries spilling from her lips, I found myself digging my hips into the mattress, needing something to alleviate the pressure that was building up inside me way too fast. If I wasn't careful, I'd blow my load before I even got inside her. And I couldn't let the first time I came be like that. Not tonight.

"God, Lennon," Hope groaned as I slipped two fingers inside her, plunging them in and out as I continued to feast on her. "Fuck, it's so good. Don't stop. *Please* don't fucking stop!"

"Not until you come for me, beautiful," I promised, grazing my teeth against her clit.

"So…close," she panted as she bucked her hips in time with my hand.

Pulling the nub back into my mouth, I curled my fingers inside her to brush against that sweet spot. And just like that, fireworks.

"*Fuck, Lennon!*" she screamed as she pulsed around my fingers, soaking my hand and face.

I didn't let up until she went limp under me, gasping for breath. And as she came down from her high, I shimmied out of my boxer briefs and crawled back up between her legs, giving her a slow kiss that I could only hope conveyed the depth of my love and joy.

"Still okay, phoenix?" I whispered against her lips.

Hope nodded. "I'm perfect."

And that was when I realized that I'd forgotten one crucial thing: protection.

"I should know this since I practically memorized your med list, but—"

"I have an implant," she supplied with a smile. "And I trust you. More than I've ever trusted anyone else in my whole life."

"Thank God," I chuckled as I feathered a kiss over her lips. "Don't let me hurt you, beautiful. Stop me if you need to."

"You won't hurt me," she murmured. "You're not capable of it. Make love to me, Lennon."

"With fucking pleasure," I breathed.

After claiming her lips for the thousandth time tonight, I rose to my knees and gave my painfully hard cock a few tugs to relieve some of the pressure. Then I lifted her good leg to tilt her hips up a little, lined myself up with her entrance, and slowly slid inside her.

"Ohmygod," she gasped as her eyes drifted to a close.

Fuck me, this sight. It was the most glorious thing I'd ever witnessed. And dear God, the way she felt. Warm and tight and squeezing me in all the right places. I swore she was made just for me.

Because she was. She was my soulmate. And I'd spend the rest of my life loving, protecting, and worshiping her.

"God, Hope," I whispered as I slowly rocked in and out of her. "You feel like heaven."

"So do you," she sighed. "Give me more, Lennon. Please. I won't break."

Leaning down to brush my lips over hers, I picked up my pace, feeling sparks of electricity race through my whole body as she met me thrust for thrust. Pressure started to build up inside me way too fast, and as much as I wanted to make this last forever, I knew I couldn't. So I slid a hand between us and used my thumb to rub circles on her clit as I tilted her hips a little more to get deeper inside her.

"Yes!" she moaned. "God, right there. Don't stop."

"Wouldn't dream of it, beautiful. I need you there with me." I drove even deeper, bottoming out with each thrust. "I know you've got another one in you."

I felt the telltale tingling at the base of my spine, telling me I was right at the edge, but I needed to get her there first. So I pressed down harder on her clit while cupping a breast in my other hand and flicking my thumb over her nipple.

"Shit!" she cried as she started to flutter around me. "Oh, fuck. I'm…gonna…*God, Lennon!*"

Her walls clutched my cock in a vise grip as her head flew back and her back arched, absolute bliss written all over her face. And that was all it took to send me over the edge with her.

"Fuck, Hope," I groaned as I spilled myself inside her.

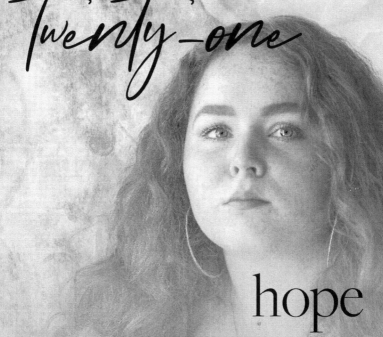

twenty-one

hope

My body was still trembling with the aftershocks of the best orgasm I'd ever had in my life as Lennon gave me a soft, tender kiss before pulling out of me.

"Oh, my God," I panted. "That was…"

I wrote this shit for a living, yet I didn't have a single word to describe the utter perfection of the past half-hour.

"Absolutely perfect. Just like you," he said softly, stealing another kiss before sitting up. "Do you have a washcloth?"

"Top left drawer of the vanity."

Lennon got up and retrieved a couple of washcloths, then went into the bathroom and wet them. He used one to clean himself off before coming to sit next to me.

"Open for me, beautiful," he murmured, putting a hand on my thigh.

I spread my legs open as much as I could, hissing as the coarse washcloth came into contact with my sensitive core. As soon as he finished cleaning me, he pulled his boxers back on and crawled back onto the bed with me, pulling me into his arms.

"I love you, phoenix," he whispered into my ear. "You're the best thing that's ever happened to me."

My lips turned up in a smile as I hummed in contentment. "I love you too."

Moving almost painfully slow, I shifted onto my side so I could face him, letting my bad leg unceremoniously flop down onto the bed. He tucked some hair behind my ear and gave me a featherlight kiss.

"How do you feel?" he asked. "Sore or anything?"

I shook my head. "Nope. I'm perfect."

Except for the fact that I'd have to sleep alone tonight after what we'd just shared. But I couldn't bring that up. Not right now. I couldn't pop the bubble yet.

"So, there's something I wanted to talk to you about if you're up for it," he said as he trailed his fingers up and down my arm.

"What is it?" I wondered.

"I hate the idea of you living here. The stairs, the slick linoleum in the kitchen and bathroom, the shower that's too small to even fit your shower chair in properly."

"I hate it here too. But I can't afford to move," I sighed. "And even if I could, it's kinda hard to go apartment hunting when you're homebound."

"I know." He leaned in and brushed a kiss on my lips. "So, at the risk of sounding like a complete lunatic and sending up a ton of red flags...what would you think about moving in with me?"

My brain slammed on the brakes so hard I got mental whiplash. Lennon had known me for a grand total of three weeks, and now he wanted me to move in with him after we'd had sex *once*?

But even though I couldn't compute *why* he'd just asked

me that, there wasn't a single alarm bell going off in my head. Nothing telling me that I needed to run far and fast. There was confusion aplenty, but no fear. Not an ounce.

"Wh…what?" was all I could manage to say.

"I know how it sounds, and I know everything's happening at lightning speed. If things were different, I wouldn't be asking this for at least a year. But I live in my grandparents' old house that I inherited when they passed last year, and it's been modified to be handicap accessible because my grandmother was in a wheelchair. It's a one-story house, it has a wheelchair ramp to the front door outside and another one in the garage, and it even has a walk-in shower with a built-in bench seat and slip-resistant flooring. And as a bonus, there are a couple of spare bedrooms that are going unused, so if you want to convert one of them to an office space where you can write and keep a stash of books and things to mail out, I'd be happy to do that for you. This isn't just because I want you with me, even though I do. So much. It's because I want you to be in a place that will help you figure out your new normal, not somewhere you have to fight every day just to survive."

I was speechless. Completely and utterly flabbergasted. Because everything he'd just described? They were all the things I'd *wished* I could have. Things I knew would make my life infinitely more livable. Not having to overcome a huge flight of stairs just to leave my damn house. Not even a couple of stairs to get from the garage to the house. A shower that wasn't a death trap. And space for an actual office to store my books and swag on top of that?

After having spent so long suffering in relative silence, I'd lost faith in the universe. I'd lost faith in everything happening for a reason, because I couldn't believe there was *any* reason that justified the hell I'd lived through. But maybe I was wrong. Maybe all of this had happened to me so I would meet Lennon. Because meeting a man who had seen me at my absolute rock bottom and fallen in love with me anyway…it couldn't have been anything other than fate.

I nodded. "Yes."

An ear-splitting grin spread across his face. "Yeah?"

"Yeah," I chuckled. "I'd have to be stupid to say no."

He kissed me breathless. "Not stupid. Cautious. But I promise you're safe with me. You can even have the second spare bedroom too if you're not comfortable sharing a bed with me yet."

"Absolutely not," I said quickly as I went for another kiss. "I honestly don't know how I'm supposed to sleep without you after tonight."

"Want to know a secret? I don't know how I'm supposed to sleep without you either. Especially after tonight."

I smiled. "Well, that makes me feel a little better about what *I* wanted to ask *you*."

"What's that?" he asked, popping a curious brow.

"How would you feel about spending the night here and meeting Peyton with me tomorrow? It's a little stupid how nervous I am about meeting her. April's coming over too, but still."

Lennon's arm circled around my waist and gently pulled me closer. "You don't have anything to be nervous about because I know she'll love you almost as much as I do. But I'd love to spend the night and meet her."

I felt a slight thud on the bed and looked to find Sydney slowly creeping up toward us. Smiling, I patted my hip, letting her know it was okay to jump up on me. Because as much of a jerk as she could be, she was also *so* cautious of hurting me. She and Vaughn both were. They could tell my right leg had issues, so unless they were deliberately trying to get my attention, they gave it a wide berth.

But to my utter shock, she jumped up on *Lennon* instead.

Sydney hated people, except for me. Especially new people. Hell, she barely tolerated April. I was the only one she snuggled with, and even that was rare. If I'd had any doubts left in my mind about whether or not I could trust Lennon, this would have put them all to rest, because I knew for a fact that she wouldn't have done that if she didn't completely trust him.

"Hey, Sydney," he chuckled, lifting his arm from me to let her sniff him before scratching behind her ears. "How do you feel about getting a whole *house* to run around in instead of this tiny apartment?"

She leaned her head into his scratches, purring loudly, and I chuckled as I reached out to pet her too.

"Did you make a new friend, sweet girl?" I cooed, then looked at Lennon. "You should feel special. She barely even lets April pet her."

I stole a quick kiss before sitting up, groaning quietly as I felt the strain in my legs and back. It wasn't unbearable, but I was definitely going to take some preemptive ibuprofen to make sure I didn't wake up stiff as a board tomorrow.

And then I realized that I didn't have my usual water bottle in here because I'd been gone for a few weeks. Turning back to Lennon, I took a deep breath.

"Would...would you mind running into the kitchen and grabbing me a thermos of water from the fridge?" I mumbled sheepishly. "I always keep a few in there. I need something to take my meds with."

"Absolutely," he said immediately, gently lifting Sydney from his chest before sitting up and kissing my shoulder. "Do you need anything else?"

I shook my head, and he gave me a quick peck before getting up and heading out of the bedroom. While he did that, I located a tank top and a pair of pajama shorts and donned them, then grabbed my small basket of meds and the pouch that housed my glucose meter, a vial of each of my two insulins, and a few syringes. After quickly checking my blood sugar, which was surprisingly low given what we'd had for dinner, I took my shot, then double-checked the humidifier tank in my CPAP machine to make sure April had filled it when she'd set the machine up for me this afternoon.

"Good thing I went out there. Vaughn was a little too interested in my guitar," Lennon chuckled as he handed the water to me and sat down, brushing his lips over my shoulder. "I had to put it back in its case."

"Crap. I completely forgot I just threw it on the coffee table before I pounced on you," I murmured, my cheeks growing warm at the delicious memories of what had come after that.

"Don't see me complaining, do you?" he teased as he got back in bed.

After swallowing my mini pharmacy of pills, I started the production of getting back into bed.

"Do you need help, beautiful?" Lennon asked after a minute or so of my grunts, groans, and struggling.

"Um…maybe?" I blew out a long, frustrated breath. "I think I need to prop my leg up. There are a couple of firm throw pillows on the couch I can use."

He hopped back up and helped me into bed, then went out to the living room and grabbed the pillows, propping my bad leg up on them. I immediately let out a sigh of relief as the pressure was taken off my back and thigh.

"Better?" he asked.

I nodded. "Thank you. I don't know how I would have managed this if you hadn't been here."

"Well, you don't have to worry about it, because I *am* here, and I'll never complain about helping you. I'll stay with you every night until you move into my house if you want me to," he said, getting back into bed *again*.

"I hate to take you up on that when the hospital is like half an hour away," I murmured.

"It's not that much farther than my place is." He planted a kiss on my cheek. "As glad as I am that you're home now, I feel like they should have done more getting resources in place for you before they transitioned you back here."

I sighed as I grabbed my CPAP mask and the remote control

off my nightstand. "I don't disagree, but their whole goal was to get me to the point where I could climb the stairs. Once I could do that, they figured I could do pretty much anything else I needed to do. But getting into a hospital bed is a whole different beast from getting into a normal bed."

"True story," he agreed.

Handing him the remote, I started fitting the mask over my nose, then reached up to flick the light off.

"Put whatever you want on," I told him. "I'm a weirdo who has to have the TV on while I sleep. I know it's supposed to be bad for you, but with my ADHD, I need it for background noise so my brain doesn't give me infinitely more annoying background noise that will make it impossible to relax enough to go to sleep. Like plotting out the next five sequels in my romantic suspense series."

He snorted as he turned on the TV and started navigating through my streaming apps, putting on the pilot episode of *Alias*. "I'm the same way, actually. After taking care of patients all day – or night, depending on what shift I'm working – I need something I don't have to think about to help me unwind."

"Stop being so perfect," I teased. "You've gotta have at least one flaw."

That made him laugh. "Let's see. I sit around doing absolutely nothing on my days off instead of doing chores. Oh, and I hate vacuuming and doing laundry."

I giggled as I shifted slightly so I could rest my head on his shoulder. He started to comb his fingers through my hair…until he realized that was an impossible feat with the oh-so-stylish headgear I was wearing.

"I know, the mask is super sexy," I grumbled. "Sorry."

He kissed my head and moved his hand to my arm, tracing invisible patterns on my skin. "You know what's sexy? You being able to breathe while you're asleep. Get some rest, phoenix. I love you. CPAP and all."

Twenty-Two

lennon

Waking up next to Hope was like something out of a dream. Feeling her head against my chest, her skin against mine…there was nothing in the world like it. And I never wanted to wake up any other way for the rest of my life. I'd never felt this kind of completeness and serenity before. Ever.

Despite the reason I woke up being a cat jumping on me and meowing loudly before moving to Hope and starting to knead her chest aggressively.

"Let your mama sleep, Vaughn," I chuckled as I tried to placate him with head scratches.

Hope let out a groggy grumble as she popped one eye open and stroked his jet-black fur. He let out a mewl as he moved his paws to her shoulder.

"Hey, buddy," she murmured as she pulled her CPAP mask

off. "Hungry? Food?"

Meow.

"I guess that's a yes," I snickered.

She giggled. "A few months after I got them, April was here and we were talking. I said the word 'food,' and I swear to God, this little piggy pig woke up from a *dead sleep*, meowed at me, then fell right back asleep. I tried it again when he was awake and it was time for his wet food, and he did it again, so it just kinda stuck."

I laughed as I grabbed him and placed him on my chest, rubbing behind his ears. "You're a smart boy, aren't you?"

Sydney chose that moment to jump up on Hope and start pacing back and forth all over her chest and stomach.

"Okay, okay," she muttered as she picked the cat up and tried to place her on the bed. "I'm coming."

But Sydney just jumped right back on her.

"You've gotta let me up if you want breakfast, silly girl," she chuckled as she once again moved Sydney to the bed, this time kicking the pillow out from under her leg and sitting up at the same time.

And then she let out a pained and frustrated groan as she tried to stand up. I quickly set Vaughn down and rushed over to kneel in front of her.

"What's wrong, beautiful?" I asked.

"My fucking leg," she mumbled, her voice cracking as she looked at the floor. "*One* goddamn day without wraps and it's already starting to get hard again. I can't bend my knee right."

Damn it. I should have thought of that last night. Hope had only just started her lymphedema wrapping, and in the early days of doing that, it didn't take the protein-based lymphatic fluid very long to re-harden when the wraps got taken off.

"It's okay, phoenix," I said softly, tilting her chin up so she'd look at me. "You're okay. Why don't you let me feed the cats, and then I'll come back in and get your leg wrapped before I find something to make for breakfast?"

"You…you know how to do lymphedema wraps?" she questioned with wide eyes.

"I'm not certified in lymphedema wrapping, but I am certified in edema wrapping, which is pretty similar. The only thing I can't do is the toe wraps."

"They never bothered with those anyway," she sighed. "Sheila tried it on the first day she wrapped me in the hospital, and they ended up getting all twisted and cutting off my circulation. I think my foot's just too swollen right now."

"Okay. So, where's the cat food? And your wrapping supplies?"

She quickly explained their food situation to me, down to the different kinds of food each cat got because Vaughn had a sensitive stomach. Then she told me where her wraps, medical tape, and the binders she used to keep her thigh wraps up were.

I gave her a slow, lingering kiss before pressing my lips to her forehead and standing up. "I'll be right back."

hope

My stomach twisted into a knot when I heard the knock on the door.

I'd known this day was coming for a week. I'd prepared for it and psyched myself up for it. And I was still utterly terrified. Because in just a few short seconds, I wouldn't be able to hide behind a phone screen anymore.

"I've got it," April said, springing up from the couch. "Since, you know, you're a mummy and all."

I let out a weak chuckle as she zipped over to the door.

"Breathe, phoenix," Lennon murmured, pulling me into his side and pressing his lips to my temple. "She loves you already. Deep breath in, then out."

I tried to match my breathing to his, and it sort of worked, but I was too keyed up for it to calm my racing heart.

As soon as April opened the door, Noah stepped inside, followed by a petite brunette with tan skin and mahogany eyes that exuded warmth and familiarity.

"Hey, sis," he said, pulling April into a one-armed hug as he closed the door behind them.

"Hey yourself," she teased, playfully elbowing her brother in the ribs before turning to his companion. "Peyton! It is *so* nice to finally put a face with a name. Do you do hugs?"

"Absolutely," Peyton chuckled nervously as she wrapped an arm around her. "It's really nice to meet you, April. I've heard so much about you from Hope, it feels like I know you already."

"Ditto," April agreed with a giggle.

Then Peyton glanced my way, and a full-blown grin broke out on her face as she rushed over to the couch and threw both arms around me in a tight hug that made my eyes sting. The bowling ball that had taken up residence in my stomach was downgraded to a tennis ball, but I still felt like I was going to throw up.

"Oh, my God, Hope," she murmured. "I'm *so* glad you're home. And I'm even gladder that I finally get to hug you for real instead of in a GIF."

I sniffled and blinked back tears as I squeezed her tight. "Same. Sorry I can't get up and hug you."

"Nope. None of that." She pulled back and looked me in the eyes as she sat on the arm of the sofa. "You literally *just* got home yesterday, and you've got your leg wrapped up like the freaking Michelin Man. I'm just happy I'm meeting you in your apartment and not a hospital room. So, are you going to introduce me to the hunk sitting next to you, or do I have to do it myself?"

Lennon laughed, and I groaned as the rest of the nerves dissipated.

"He can hear you, you know," I snickered.

"I know, but I got a laugh out of you," she teased. "So?"

"Lennon, this is Peyton, my other best friend besides April, who I've never met in person before now. Pey, this is my boyfriend, Lennon, otherwise known as the night nurse who did *not* give me sponge baths."

Everyone in the room started cracking up, and Lennon pulled me into his arms and stole a kiss.

"You realize a sponge bath is in your future now, right, beautiful?" he whispered into my ear.

"Only if it comes with a happy ending," I breathed back.

"Abso-fucking-lutely," he groaned quietly, nipping at my earlobe.

"Okay, who's hungry?" April asked. "I made a huge batch of grape tomato, feta, and orzo salad yesterday, and we've got a smorgasbord of stuff for sandwiches too. And Peyton, I got you some saltines and ginger ale if you need it."

"I'd actually love to try eating real food," she said. "Since I'm feeling somewhat normal today. But I will take a ginger ale."

"There's leftover carrot cake in the fridge too," Lennon offered. "The only one they had at the bakery yesterday was fucking *massive*, but I figured we could have the rest today."

"Sweet." April grinned. "Feel like giving me a hand with everything?"

"Yep," he said, then turned to me. "You okay if I help April, phoenix?"

I nodded. "I'm good. Thanks."

He got up and started for the kitchen, pausing to kiss the top of my head. I took a second to admire the way his jeans hugged his ass before turning back to Peyton.

"Girl, you've got it bad," she chuckled. "But it's good to see you so happy. I guess this means your stay-in date went well last night?"

"Oh, my God, yes," I gushed. "He, um…he spent the night. And he also asked me to move in with him."

Her eyes bugged out. "Say *what* now? You've known each

other…what, less than a month? And he's already asking you to move in? Tell me you didn't say yes."

Crap. I'd completely forgotten that was what Michael had done to her. He'd moved fast – too fast – and she'd been so swept up in the love-bombing that she hadn't even questioned it. Until it was too late.

"It's not like that," I said quickly. "It's because this whole apartment complex is basically a giant death trap for me. He inherited his grandparents' house when they died last year, and his grandmother was in a wheelchair, so the whole house is handicap accessible. It's one-story with wheelchair ramps for the front door and the one inside the garage, and it has a walk-in shower with a bench and slip-resistant floors. He even told me I could sleep in one of the spare bedrooms if I wanted. He just wants me to be in a place that's more suited to my needs. Because like it or not, this is my new normal."

"Okay, that actually makes sense," she sighed, sounding relieved. "In that case, I approve."

I let out a chuckle. Now that I'd gotten past the awkward introductions with Peyton, I was surprised to find that the easy friendship we'd had online was the same in person. I'd never been very good at peopling, but with her, just like with April and Lennon, it didn't feel like I *was* peopling. Rather than draining my social battery, talking to her recharged it.

"I was so nervous to meet you today," I admitted.

"I could tell," she said, rubbing my arm with a sympathetic smile. "I'd like to think I know you pretty well after the past couple of years. And I knew why you were nervous, but I didn't want to say anything until we actually met in person because I didn't want your anxiety spiking any more than it already was. Hope, you saved my life. You were always there for me, day or night, letting me talk and vent and tell you every godawful thing that son of a bitch did to me without pushing me to leave him, but then you immediately jumped to my rescue when I was ready to get out. You are absolutely gorgeous inside *and* out, but

I wouldn't have cared if you looked like an orc. Because what I see when I look at you is quite literally the *only* person who really knows me and has never judged me. And that's why you, missy, are stuck with me for life."

She gave me another hug, and I took slow, deep breaths to keep myself from bursting into tears. This was a happy day, and I refused to ruin it with yet *another* cryfest.

"You're stuck with me too, phoenix," Lennon said as he walked back into the living room with a stack of plates in one hand and the huge Tupperware bowl of the orzo salad in the other. He set everything on the coffee table, then pulled me into his arms and kissed my head. "Told you she'd love you."

Peyton smiled at us. "Okay, I have to know. Phoenix?"

I snorted. "Well, do you want the dorky version or the super sweet version?"

"Um, both? Duh," she giggled.

"Dorky version? It was Sydney's code name in the last couple of seasons of *Alias*." I felt my cheeks heating.

"But I only realized that after I said it the first time," he added. "The real reason is because she's a fighter. Like a phoenix rising from the ashes."

"Oh, my God," she said as her smile got even bigger. "That's adorable and I love it."

"Okay, can you two *not* be so damn cute?" Noah teased from the seat he'd found on the floor.

"Be nice, dude," April scoffed as she set a huge tray of sandwich fixings on the coffee table and sat next to him. "That's my bestie you're insulting."

"What? I *am* being nice," he protested. "I just said they were cute."

"Yeah, by asking them *not* to be cute."

I rolled my eyes, chuckling. And as I sat here, surrounded by people who loved and accepted me exactly as I was, with no strings attached, I realized that everything absolutely happened for a reason.

Yeah, maybe my new normal wasn't the life I had once envisioned. Maybe I would never be fully mobile again and I'd have to make some adjustments. But that was okay, because at the end of the day, this new normal had blessed me with an amazing friendship that I knew would last a lifetime. And it had sent me a man who had seen me at my very worst and loved me for exactly who I was, imperfections and all.

epilogue

lennon
three weeks later

Note: The song "Hanging by a Moment" by Lifehouse plays a significant role in this chapter. If you don't know it, I highly recommend listening to it to get the full effect.

As I pulled into the parking lot at Northwest Rehabilitation, I looked over at Hope, who looked like she was about to shit a brick.

"You okay, beautiful?" I asked her.

"It's weird being back here," she mumbled, taking a deep breath. "But at least this time I get to leave in a couple of hours."

I smiled and pulled her into a kiss. "Yep. And when you do, you get to come home to a place where it isn't a major production just to get in the door."

I'd moved Hope into my house last weekend, with the

help of Brady, Noah, Peyton, and April. I'd also paid the early termination fee to the apartment complex so she didn't have to worry about finding someone to sublet until her lease was up. From the second she'd walked in the door – using the ramp to get into the house from the garage – I'd known it was the right call. She'd actually cried when she was able to get inside and walk to the couch without needing to take a break or being completely spent at the end of it.

Sydney and Vaughn were still getting used to being in a new space, but I knew they could see how much happier their mama was in the house. And the new cat tree I'd bought them, which was twice the size of their old one, seemed to be an acceptable peace offering for uprooting them from the only home they'd ever known. They spent more time on that thing than off it.

"So, you ready to meet my sister?" I asked.

She nodded. "Ready as I'll ever be."

"Just remember, you're one of her favorite authors," I chuckled. "The second you give her those books and swag, she'll be your new best friend."

She let out a nervous giggle, and I pecked her lips before getting out and grabbing her wheelchair out of the back. After helping her out of the car and getting her situated, I handed her my guitar case, which she held on her lap, while hanging the gift bag containing the books she'd signed for Star on one of the handles of the chair.

My sister's eyes got as big as saucers when I wheeled Hope into her room.

"Oh. My. God," she squealed. "Um, Lennon, why the hell didn't you tell me that your girlfriend was *Hope freaking Claire*?!"

I laughed. "HIPPA's still a thing, remember? She was my patient when I first told you about her."

"Yeah, but…oh, my God!"

Hope let out a nervous chuckle. "Sorry for springing my alter ego on you like this. I honestly didn't think you'd recognize me. The picture on my Facebook page is a few years old. But… since Lennon told me how much you love my books, I brought something for you."

After pushing the wheelchair next to the bed, I took my guitar from Hope and handed her the gift bag, which she immediately gave to Star.

"Gah! *Accidentally in Love*! This one's my *favorite*," Star gushed. "And the *Second Chances in Hampton* books! Oh, my God! A squishy peen! I've been wanting one of these *forever*! Thank you!"

I snorted. Those little phallus-shaped squishy toys were hilarious.

"*Oookay,* are you done fangirling now?" I groaned.

"Yep. I'm done. I'm sorry. It's really nice to meet you, Hope," she said with a grin. "Wait, is that even your real name?"

"It's nice to finally meet you too," Hope murmured. "Lennon's told me so much about you. And yes, my name's really Hope. Hope Morrison. Claire is my middle name, after my grandma."

"Do I get to ask how you started writing? Or is that still fangirling?" she asked, smirking at me.

Hope giggled. "No, you can ask. Um, long story short, I have lymphedema, my leg decided it hated me, and it got so bad I had to go on disability. So I started writing just to have something to do and discovered I loved it. And here I am now."

"That's amazing. I have a story I started before my accident. I keep thinking I might want to pick it back up, but then I get scared that too much time has passed, you know?"

"You should absolutely pick it back up. Maybe you'll end up rewriting parts of it or that story won't speak to you anymore, but especially when you've had something traumatic happen to you, it can be *so* cathartic to get those emotions out through your characters. Even though my characters' stories and journeys and pain are different from mine, I put a little bit of myself into every story I write, and it just helps to purge those feelings and then let my characters come out stronger on the other side."

My heart swelled with pride as I grabbed Hope's hand and brought it to my lips. "Just like you did."

Hope turned to me with a soft smile. "I wouldn't have if it hadn't been for you. You helped me survive the hell I went through. I hope you know that."

Standing halfway, I leaned in and brushed my lips against hers. "We helped each other, phoenix. Because you brought me back to life."

"Aww," Star murmured. "You two are adorable together. Have you ever thought about writing your story, Hope? I mean, the way you and my brother met is like something out of a romcom."

Hope flushed crimson, and I smiled as I kissed her forehead before sitting back down and getting my guitar out of its case.

"I don't know," she sighed. "Maybe one day. But I think it's still a little too raw right now. My life hasn't exactly been romcom material. Not until recently."

"I get that. But just know that I'd read the hell out of it if you did decide to. And that you absolutely get my seal of approval. I haven't seen Lennon this happy in a long time." Star glanced at me as I tuned my guitar. "And now it seems like we've arrived at the singalong portion of today's visit."

I laughed. "Only if you want it to be the singalong portion. But since you've seemed to enjoy said singalongs lately…"

"I *have* enjoyed them. Please, continue." She made a sweeping gesture with her hand.

"You're the boss," I teased.

I played a few random chords as I tried to decide what to play. And when I looked over at Hope, I had my answer. As I played Lifehouse's "Hanging by a Moment," I couldn't help reflecting on how much my life had changed in such a short time.

Two months ago, I'd been an empty shell of a man. Unable to let go, to move on from the trauma and grief that consumed me. But now, while I still carried that pain with me and was still working through it in therapy, I wasn't crippled by the loss I'd suffered anymore. I was able to look ahead to the future.

And that future had never looked so bright. Because right there at the center of it was the woman I was falling more and more in love with every day. My phoenix, risen from the ashes.

bonus epilogue

hope
eighteen months later

I felt like I was going to throw up.

I had absolutely no idea why my agoraphobic, social-anxiety-ridden ass had agreed to be a signing author at a book convention. I sucked at peopling, and I was about to have to people *all damn day.*

Okay, I knew why. I'd agreed because Lennon, April, Star, Peyton, and Noah had all ganged up on me and encouraged me to do it. And because my most recent release, *Hope Rekindled* – the book I'd written that was loosely based on Lennon and I's story – had hit a couple of bestseller lists after a BookTok video about it had gone viral.

It was still nerve-wracking, though. Because I couldn't hide behind a screen of relative anonymity and a five-year-old photo anymore.

What if people took one look at me and were immediately disgusted by what they saw? What if my book sales started to tank after someone made a post about the fat, hideous author who had the audacity to write romance novels? What if someone actually said something about my weight or my leg to my face?

Okay, I knew Lennon and Peyton wouldn't let that fly and would personally deal with it even if security didn't get involved, but still. It was a possibility. People were cruel.

"You ready to do this, phoenix?" Lennon asked as he pulled up to the curb at the convention center, pulling me out of the downward spiral my thoughts had started to go into.

"No. But there's no going back now, is there?" I sighed.

He smiled and pulled me into a kiss that I felt all the way down to my bones. "You don't have to do *anything* you don't want to do, beautiful. But remember, you have people who love you here."

He pulled his phone out and tapped on the screen for a few seconds, then got out of the car and grabbed my wheelchair out of the back.

Even though the size of my leg had gone down significantly and my mobility had improved a lot, my health would never be what it was before this had all started, and I knew that. So, when it came to things like this where I knew there would be a lot of ground to cover and there were also a lot of unknowns about things like the distance from where I was going to be sitting to the nearest restroom, I still used my chair. There was no need to put my body under completely unnecessary stress.

"There's the woman of the hour!" Peyton exclaimed as she walked out of the building just as Lennon was locking my leg rests – with her eleven-month-old daughter, Dove, wrapped snugly on her back. "*Please* tell me you made her eat something this morning, Lennon."

"You bet I did," he assured her. "Brought some snacks for all of us too."

"Extra muscle reporting for duty. Whatcha need?" Noah asked, right on her heels.

Peyton turned to beam at him, and I smiled as a little bit of my anxiety melted away. It warmed my heart to see her *finally* getting her own happily ever after. Her love story with Noah was one for the ages, and she'd toyed with the idea of writing it. I'd promised to help her every step of the way if she decided to, but right now, she was just focusing on being a mom to that precious little girl.

Today, though? She was here as my personal assistant. After my books had taken off and I'd been able to afford to pay her, I'd immediately hired her as my PA, and I honestly didn't know where I'd be without her. She kept my whole life, not just my author schedule, organized. Noah was here to help with the setup, and then he was going to take Dove home and Lennon and I would give Peyton a ride after the event was over.

"Can you stay here with the totes and banner?" Lennon asked Noah. "I'll come help you bring it all in after I park."

"Sure thing," he said immediately.

Then Lennon reached into the backseat and grabbed the cooler he'd brought with some snacks and drinks since this was an all-day event and we didn't get a lunch break, hanging it on the handlebars of my chair. And finally, he gave me the two gift baskets I'd brought – one to give away at my table, and one to donate to the charity raffle that the people who were organizing this event were putting on – plus the swag I'd put together for the VIP bags.

"Pey, do you know where I'm supposed to deliver this basket and swag?" I asked.

"Yep. I already scoped it out," she assured me. "I've got your back."

"You ladies go on inside and drop that stuff off where it needs to go. We'll be there soon to help with the table setup," Lennon told us.

"Sir, yes, sir." Peyton gave him a mock salute, then grabbed my wheelchair handles. "Let's do this thing, woman!"

"Oh, my God. That banner looks so good!" Star exclaimed as she wheeled herself up to my table right after the doors opened for the VIP ticketholders.

Like me, she'd come leaps and bounds in her recovery – and was actually living with April now – but she still needed her wheelchair anytime serious walking was involved.

"Right? This new logo is amazing, if I do say so myself," I agreed.

A few months ago, I'd decided to do a rebrand of my pen name, using Lennon's favorite endearment for me as inspiration. The image was a phoenix surrounded by a ring of fire, accompanied by a brand new tagline: *Love that burns eternal.*

April walked up next to her, grinning as she looked at the table setup. "This whole *table* looks amazing. Good work, guys."

"It's perfect. For you and your stories," Star said with a smile as she grabbed a pin featuring said new logo and a ribbon to add to her badge. "And I'mma need one of those shirts you guys are wearing, please and thank you."

"Me too," April said. "I'm not above begging."

"We thought you might say that." Lennon chuckled, reaching under the table for the shirts we'd had made for the two of them. "One for each of you. But hide them in your bags for now, because they're the only other two in existence."

"Have you thought about setting up a merch shop online?" Star asked. "You could use your logo for some stuff, like these shirts, and also maybe make some items with things from your books. Like that coffee shop in the Hampton duet, or even just your favorite quotes."

"We've talked about it," Peyton told her. "But she wanted to get through this signing before she did that. She didn't want to spread herself too thin. And what needs to go on a shirt is Jimmy the scam guy and his grandma."

I started cracking up, because out of that dumb predictive text game response, she and I had jokingly created a whole backstory about the scam guy – who we'd affectionately named Jimmy – and his grandma, who were running a Ponzi scheme. I'd even snuck them into my semi-autobiographical book.

"I still don't get what's so funny about that," April chuckled.

"You had to be there," I snickered.

"Oh, my God," a middle-aged woman with dark tan skin said as she approached the table. "I'm so glad you're here! I just finished reading *Hope Rekindled*, and I absolutely *loved* it. Please tell me you have some extra copies of that one, because I didn't get a chance to pre-order it."

"We'll see you guys later," Star said, then turned to April. "Come on, baby. Let's go mingle."

"Bye, girls," I said, then turned to the woman, who was patiently waiting. "Sorry about that. I absolutely have extras of *Hope Rekindled*. The discreet cover was pre-order only, but I've got plenty of the model cover. It's fifteen."

"Sold," she said as she handed Lennon – who was on cashier duty – a twenty.

While he handed her change back to her, I grabbed a copy of the book and my new sparkly orange Sharpie to sign with, opening it to the title page.

"What's your name?"

"Talia," she said with a grin. "Do you mind taking a picture with me?"

"Not at all. I'm in a wheelchair, though, so you'll have to come back here."

"I can take it if you pull up your camera," Peyton offered.

Handing Peyton her phone, Talia rounded the table and bent down so she was at my level as she snapped the photo. Then I handed her the signed book and a swag pack that included some extra goodies for people who actually bought something from me, and she thanked me and left.

"See? I told you people would love you," Peyton said, squeezing my shoulder as Talia walked away.

Maybe this event wouldn't be so horrible after all.

It had been a *long* day. Long, but worth it.

I didn't know if I'd ever end up traveling long distances to do a signing because my health issues made travel difficult, but I definitely wasn't opposed to the idea of doing more local ones. I'd gotten to meet so many amazing people, readers and authors alike.

There was about an hour to go, and while there were still people milling around, the mayhem had died down.

"Pey, do you mind taking over for me for a minute?" Lennon asked as the last person in my line walked away. "I'll be right back."

"Absolutely." An ear-splitting grin spread across her face as she walked over to his chair.

He got up and planted a kiss on my head, then walked away...in the exact opposite direction of where the bathrooms were. What the hell else could he have been doing?

I turned to look at Peyton, narrowing my eyes at her. "Okay, what do you know? Because you look *way* too happy right now."

She snorted. "I can't just be glad this has gone so well? This is a huge deal for you, Hope. I know you had *so* much anxiety about coming today, but you did it anyway and everyone loved you."

Just as I opened my mouth to say something, I heard the opening chords of "Hold on Forever," and I turned around to find Lennon walking back toward the table as he started to sing.

Oh. My. God. Was what I thought was happening right now actually happening?

"Is...is he allowed..." I started.

Peyton laughed and hugged my shoulders. "They knew, silly. He emailed them *weeks* ago to ask if it was okay."

As Lennon continued to play the song, coming to stand right in front of me, a small crowd congregated around us. But I couldn't have peeled my eyes away from him if my life depended on it. Because his eyes – those gorgeous brown depths I loved so much – were shining with pure love and joy as he sang to me about holding on through the good times and the bad.

When the song was over, he pulled the guitar strap over his head and passed the instrument to Peyton before retrieving a small velvet box from his pocket and dropping to one knee.

"Hope, when I met you, we were both at the lowest points of our lives, and neither one of us could see the light in the darkness. Until we found each other. From the second I met you, something drew me in, and even though I didn't understand it, I knew I had to know you. I fell hard and fast, and every single day I spend with you, I still find something new to fall in love with. Something new to hold on to. So…"

He opened the box to reveal a beautiful yellow gold ring with a round-cut diamond in the center and pavé diamond infinity symbols on either side of it.

"Today, I want to ask you to hold on to me – to *us* – forever. Will you marry me, phoenix?"

I swallowed the lump in my throat and swiped at the tears forming in my eyes. "Yes. Yes, of course!"

He beamed at me with a smile that could have lit up Times Square as he took the ring out of the box. But before he put it on my finger, he held it up so I could see the engraving inside.

Hold on forever.

As I bent down to kiss the man I loved, the man who had proven time and again that he was here through thick and thin, through good times and bad, a chorus of cheers erupted around us.

And I barely heard a thing. Because right now, in this moment, it was just me and him. Holding on to each other forever.

The end

cinnamon roll

saviors

Cinnamon Roll Hero (sin-a-mon roll he-ro): (n) a hero who is too sweet for this world…but will fight to the death for the people they care about.

Join nineteen of your favorite romance authors on our journey to prove that cinnamon rolls can still be steaming hot! These sweet, sexy heroes (and heroines!) are here to save the day, whether it's rescuing their partner from the ghosts of their past or just showing them that they deserve to be loved, cherished, respected…and, of course, pleasured.

Check out the whole series at **https://mybook.to/ CinnamonRollSaviors**. Or check out the individual books here:

- *Taking Her* by Stormi Wilde
- *Burning Love* by Ember Davis
- *Indebted Angel* by Clarissa Dusk
- *Have a Little Faith* by Stephanie Renee
- *Second Time Lucky* by Mia Coco Lanner
- *Sidelined* by Sarah Everly
- *Keeping Her Safe* by Lyric Nicole
- *Safety* by JS Mercier
- *Only to Save You* by Shannon O'Connor
- *Power Play* by Merissa Bartlett
- *Matched With the Billionaire* by Sara Hurst
- *Running After You* by Cristina Lollabrigida

- *It Had to Be You* by Danielle Jacks
- *Guarding Her Heart* by Tamrin Banks
- *One Night With a Rock Star* by Eve London
- *Protecting What's His* by Aletta Faye
- *Falling for My Sweet Saviour* by Clarice Jayne
- *Patient 247* by Carmen Richter
- *Inked Temptations* by Storie Devereux

playlist

As I tried to build my playlist for this story, it started as songs that had the general themes of what I was writing about: overcoming adversity, seeing someone's true colors and falling in love with them because of that, and perhaps most importantly, learning to love yourself. It was an amazing, uplifting playlist, with a few angsty songs to represent how Hope feels toward the beginning of the story, and I started listening to it while plotting my story.

And then my characters shut up on me. They refused to talk at all, and everything I tried to write turned out horrible.

I'm ashamed to say it took me a *lot* longer to figure out what the problem was than it should have. It was the music. So, I deleted seventy-five percent of the songs I'd carefully selected for this story and started fresh…with a bunch of songs that won't make sense to anyone but me.

If you read the foreword, you know that this story is painstakingly personal to me because it's a fictionalized version of an extremely painful time in my life. And what I needed as I wrote Hope's story was the music that helped me survive when I went through what she endured in this book (and continues to help me as I navigate my new normal as a disabled person). If you've ever wondered why so many of my playlists have a ton of Goo Goo Dolls and Rob Thomas/Matchbox Twenty on them, this is why. It's because they're the artists that helped me the most when I hit rock bottom. I'm not kidding when I say I owe my life to the songs on this playlist.

And guess what? As soon as I started listening to these songs, Hope and Lennon started screaming and writing the story was…

well, not effortless, but a lot easier than it had been before.

If you're so inclined to listen to a bunch of dad rock (because, really, would you have expected anything else from me?) and a smattering of other random songs that spoke to me, you can do it at **https://bit.ly/Patient247Playlist**. And if you do, I can only hope that some of this music touches you the way it's touched me.

- "Crazy Train" by Ozzy Osbourne
- "Unwell" by Matchbox Twenty
- "Disease" by Matchbox Twenty
- "Bright Lights" by Matchbox Twenty
- "Push" by Matchbox Twenty
- "Back 2 Good" by Matchbox Twenty
- "3AM" by Matchbox Twenty
- "Real World" by Matchbox Twenty
- "If You're Gone" by Matchbox Twenty
- "Bent" by Matchbox Twenty
- "Mad Season" by Matchbox Twenty
- "She's So Mean" by Matchbox Twenty
- "Little Wonders" by Rob Thomas
- "Lonely No More" by Rob Thomas
- "Streetcorner Symphony" by Rob Thomas
- "I Think We'd Feel Good Together" by Rob Thomas
- "Hold on Forever" by Rob Thomas
- "Pieces" by Rob Thomas
- "Give Me the Meltdown" by Rob Thomas
- "Someday" by Rob Thomas
- "Real World '09" by Rob Thomas
- "Fire on the Mountain" by Rob Thomas
- "Can't Help Me Now" by Rob Thomas
- "The Worst in Me" by Rob Thomas
- "Tomorrow" by Rob Thomas
- "Slide" by Goo Goo Dolls
- "Black Balloon" by Goo Goo Dolls

- "Acoustic #3" by Goo Goo Dolls
- "Iris" by Goo Goo Dolls
- "Big Machine" by Goo Goo Dolls
- "Sympathy" by Goo Goo Dolls
- "Name – New Version" by Goo Goo Dolls
- "Let Love In" by Goo Goo Dolls
- "Better Days" by Goo Goo Dolls
- "Rebel Beat" by Goo Goo Dolls
- "When the World Breaks Your Heart" by Goo Goo Dolls
- "Come to Me" by Goo Goo Dolls
- "Home" by Goo Goo Dolls
- "Still Your Song" by Goo Goo Dolls
- "Notbroken" by Goo Goo Dolls
- "Home" by Daughtry
- "Waiting for Superman" by Daughtry
- "I'll Fight" by Daughtry
- "Hanging by a Moment" by Lifehouse
- "The Middle" by Jimmy Eat World
- "Hold On" by Wilson Phillips
- "Brave" by Josh Groban
- "More of You" by Josh Groban
- "(You Make Me Feel Like) A Natural Woman" by Aretha Franklin
- "TRUSTFALL" by P!nk
- "F**kin' Perfect" by P!nk
- "All I Know So Far" by P!nk
- "We Are Never Ever Getting Back Together" by Taylor Swift
- "You Belong With Me" by Taylor Swift

acknowledgments

Oh, my God. I did it. I actually finished this story. Right under the wire, but it's done.

And I couldn't be prouder of it. But, as usual, it took a village to make this book happen. So this is my opportunity to thank all the people who kept me sane, held me accountable, and pushed me to make Hope and Lennon's story the very best it could be.

Brittany: My chosen sister, work wife, rockstar PA, and alpha reader extraordinaire. This book would *not* have been finished on time if it hadn't been for you. You took everything you possibly could off my shoulders – and almost singlehandedly ran this collab toward the end – so I could focus on writing. I am so, SOOOOO grateful for you. You will NEVER know how much. Thank you for reading every single word of this book. Thank you for loving my stories like a trash panda loves dumpsters (yes, I stole that line from you). And thank you for being such an amazing friend and letting me vent and cry and vent and cry some more while I was writing this story.

Katey: My other chosen sister, Wonder Alpha, and fabulous proofreader. Jimmy the scam guy and his grandma (who is still SOOOOOOO friggin' proud) have finally been forever immortalized in print! LMAO!!! Thank you for alpha reading most of this book, for proofreading the whole thing, and for pushing me to write about the tough stuff. Because, as usual, you were right. All those painful memories I kept buried so deep made the story that much stronger. But more than any of that, THANK YOU for being there for me when all the awfulness Hope went through happened to me. Words don't exist to tell you how much your friendship has meant to me these past few years.

Mandie: Yet another chosen sibling! Thank you for being you, for encouraging me to stick with this story, and for putting up with me being such a horribly uncommunicative friend these past couple of months. It all paid off, just like you kept telling me it would!

Jenn: And yet another chosen sister! Thank you for reading the first few chapters of this story and assuring me it didn't suck, and for pushing me to keep going! I'm so glad I met you on BookTok last year!!!

Brett: My real-life Lennon. Thank you for putting up with the late nights, meltdowns, and stress of the past few months as I struggled to find the words to tell my story right. Thank you for holding on to me forever (and yes, I'm using a Rob Thomas reference even though you don't like him – HA!), through all the pain and trauma of this godawful condition. I love you more than I know how to tell you.

Lauren Tisdale: Thank you SO much for helping me title *100 Reasons I Loved You*! I may or may not have a very loose idea for that book now. ;-)

Liz Sanchez: Thank you for naming Candace for me! And for loving my stories so much. It's readers like you that make this doing this author thing worth it.

Stormi, Ember, Clarissa, Stephanie, Mia, Sarah, Lyric, J.S., Shannon, Merissa, Sara, Cristina, Danielle, Tamrin, Eve, Aletta, Clarice, and Storie: My fellow *Cinnamon Roll Saviors* authors! Thank you all for making my first time running a collaboration go so smoothly and for being patient with me as we dealt with the small hiccups. The success of this series is ALL thanks to you!!!

You: Yes, you. Thank you so much for giving Hope and Lennon's unconventional story a chance. I hope you ended up loving them as much as I do, and that you'll check out some of my other stories that aren't quite as personal as this one (though

I do still come for my glass of salty tears with every single one of my stories). If you did love it (or if you hated it…but if you hated it, I'm guessing you wouldn't have gotten this far), I'd really appreciate it if you'd leave an honest review on your favorite book review site. Thanks, and I'll see you next book!

Much love,
Carmen

also by carmen richter

Eagle Security SERIES
Angsty, Steamy Bodyguard Romance

1. *Falling Angel* (Female Rock Star Romantic Suspense)
2. *Falling to Pieces* (Female Rock Star Age Gap Romance
   - COMING 2024)

DeVille Records SERIES
Steamy, Low-Angst Female Rock Star Romance Novellas

1. *Sing Noelle* (Friends-to-Lovers Christmas Romance)
2. *Keeping Bailey* (Long-Distance Online Romance)
3. *Accidental Love* (F/F Rock Star/Manager Romance)
4. *Choosing Cassidy* (Age Gap Musician/Tour Manager
   Romance - COMING 2024)

Lake Serenity Series
Steamy, Low-Angst Small Town Romance

1. *Mistletoe & Holly* (Single Mom Winter Romance)

Game of Love SERIES
Angsty, Steamy New Adult Sports Romance

1. *Breaking My Silence* (Friends-to-Lovers Hurt/Comfort
   Romantic Suspense)

2. *Under My Skin* (Secret Baby [with a twist!] Fake Relationship Romance - COMING 2023)

Sealed With a Kiss SERIES
Angsty, Steamy Small Town Romance
*Indicates title is part of Zoe's continuous trilogy
**Indicates title is part of Elijah's continuous trilogy

1. *My Vows Are Sealed* (Coming-of-Age First Love Abuse Rescue Romance)
2. *My Lips Are Sealed** (Student/Teacher Hurt/Comfort Romance)
3. *My Heart Is Sealed** (Hurt/Comfort Romantic Suspense)
4. *My Future Is Sealed** (Hurt/Comfort Romantic Suspense)
5. *My Fate Is Sealed*** (Student/Teacher Hurt/Comfort Romance)
6. *My Bonds Are Sealed* (Friends-to-Lovers Hurt/Comfort Romance)
7. *My Soul Is Sealed*** (Hurt/Comfort Romantic Suspense)
8. *My Dreams Are Sealed*** (Hurt/Comfort Romantic Suspense)
9. *My Pride Is Sealed* (F/F Hurt/Comfort Romance)
10. *My Voice Is Sealed* (Stepsibling Abuse Rescue Romance)

STANDALONE

1. *Zone Defense* (Second Chance Pro Football Romance Novella - ties in w/ *Game of Love* series)
2. *Patient 247* (Nurse/Patient Hurt/Comfort Romance)

CARMEN RICHTER

REAL ISSUES. REAL CONNECTIONS. REAL ROMANCE.

Carmen Richter is an old soul. Her words are like theater, masterfully spun to bring all the feels, interspersed with music that makes your heart soar. She needs her coffee to make the words flow, and some of her best writing is done in a caffeine-induced haze at one in the morning. Carmen lives in Kansas City with her boyfriend, Brett, and their two fur babies, a bunny named Marty and a cat named Mal. When she's not writing or editing, she loves going to concerts and live theater, or just binging *Criminal Minds* or *SVU* for the umpteenth time.

In addition to writing, Carmen also has an editing, proofreading, and formatting business called CPR Editing, which aims to provide quality, affordable editing and formatting to all indie authors, and a graphic design business called CPR Designs that does logos and branding, covers, teasers, and social media graphics.

Carmen loves interacting with her fans and will happily respond to all messages personally until she gets uber famous and gets a ton of them. Hey, a girl can dream, right?

You can find Carmen online in the following places:

Website: www.carmenrichterwriting.com
Newsletter: www.subscribepage.com/carmenrichter
Patreon: www.patreon.com/cprwriting
Facebook Page: www.facebook.com/carmenrichterwriting
Richter's Romance Readers (Facebook Reader Group):
www.facebook.com/groups/richtersromancereaders
Instagram/Twitter/TikTok: @cprwriting

Amazon Author Page:
www.amazon.com/author/carmenrichter
Goodreads Author Page:
www.goodreads.com/carmenrichter
BookBub Author Page:
www.bookbub.com/authors/carmen-richter
AllAuthor Author Page:
www.allauthor.com/author/carmenrichter

Also, if you enjoyed this book, please take a moment to leave an honest review on your favorite book review site. Thanks, and happy reading!

Made in the USA
Columbia, SC
12 November 2024